Revolution: 80 Days

Arius Lauren Raposas

Ukiyoto Publishing

All global publishing rights are held by

Ukiyoto Publishing

Published in 2022

Content Copyright © Arius Lauren Raposas

ISBN 9789359209821

All rights reserved.
No part of this publication may be reproduced, transmitted, or stored in a retrieval system, in any form by any means, electronic, mechanical, photocopying, recording or otherwise, without the prior permission of the publisher.

The moral rights of the author have been asserted.

This is a work of fiction. Names, characters, businesses, places, events, locales, and incidents are either the products of the author's imagination or used in a fictitious manner. Any resemblance to actual persons, living or dead, or actual events is purely coincidental.

This book is sold subject to the condition that it shall not by way of trade or otherwise, be lent, resold, hired out or otherwise circulated, without the publisher's prior consent, in any form of binding or cover other than that in which it is published.

Dedication

To the Almighty God, who has given everything that He has willed to provide at my disposal. From family support to friendly aid, this individual work would have not been possible without the Lord's benevolent sovereignty over our lives.

Contents

Introduction	1
Unfinished Revolution	3
Hello World	19
Fail Early	35
Power Failure	53
Strengthen Thyself	69
Auspicious Return	88
Nation Aborted	110
Abondoned Hope	128
Winter Soldier	148
Enduring Freedom	167
Treaty Trap	191
Ascendant Celebrity	211
Captive Philosophy	226
Epilogue: Cruel Angel's Thesis	241
About the Author	244

Introduction

They say a revolution usually took 365 days, but could it be possible in just eighty? British gentleman Phileas Fogg drove the world crazy with his uncanny wager to circumnavigate the globe in eighty days, at the wake of the infamous robbery done against the Bank of England. His sensational adventure, however, came to a grim end on his part as he became 20,000 pounds poorer after finishing the journey on the 81st day. The slim loss, meanwhile, did not seem to discourage the populace from proving him right. The following year, 1873, was met with a daring public declaration from two ladies and one gentleman to fulfill the monumental task, this time through an even heftier wager that tripled Fogg's stakes.

The lone gentleman who stepped up was one of Fogg's few friends remaining in the Reform Club, the similarly eccentric yet relatively unknown Richard Haze. Intent on redeeming his friend's convictions and taking his own place in history even as his prosperity was placed on the line, Haze decided to acquire the services of a valet who had sufficient experience and knowledge of the other side of the world in order to avoid Fogg's fate. He found the person in the Filipino migrant worker Juan Ruiz, who beneath his cheerful façade as a valet, and his limited grasp of the English and Spanish languages was a closely held secret – he was the real bank thief.

Indefinitely detained in London due to utmost diligence of the police force, the disguised Ruiz now found in Haze's wager a legitimate way for him to escape the country and accomplish the next phase of his ultimate mission. That is, bringing the money to the Philippines in order to fund a revolution there and avenge the failure of the 1872 Cavite Mutiny, an event engraved not only in the archipelago's history, but also in Ruiz's personal memory. With both men bent on their respective paths towards redemption and revolution, how would this affect the ever-changing world around them? In an era of brewing instability, how could victory be assured?

Disclaimer: This is a work of fiction. Names, characters, places, institutions, events, incidents, and other aspects of the story are merely products of the author's imagination. Any resemblance to actual persons, living or dead, actual places, actual institutions, or actual events, historical or current, are purely coincidental. Opinions and views expressed by the characters do not necessarily reflect the author's preferences. Certain real-world references and mentions do not indicate any departure from the fictitious nature of this work.

Unfinished Revolution

"The final secret sword, La Luz del Mundo!"

As his moustache quivered when he spoke the words, the exhausted yet extraordinarily spirited Sergeant Fernando Lamadrid tightened the grip of his sabre upon gazing at the advancing government forces. Some of the 200 Filipino and Spanish soldiers and laborers with him taking over Cavite's Fort San Felipe have already fallen due to the opponent's immense military advantage. With no hope of reinforcements coming and with supplies running low, their mutiny holding the stone fortress seemed on the verge of inevitable collapse.

Witnessing the drop in morale prompted the sergeant leading them to pierce through enemy lines himself. Slashing and cutting through every loyalist Spanish he could find, his fellow mutineers looked on from behind, hesitant to leave the fort in order to aid their valiant leader. Instantaneously, smoke filled the grounds, the bloodied Lamadrid disappearing from their sight. This caused worry for everyone in the rebel ranks, except one.

Abandoning his pistol, the smiling mutineer Francisco Saldua decided to take advantage of the situation and flee the scene without anybody else knowing. Unfortunately for him, a keen corporal managed to spot his attempt to make a break for it. The agitated corporal grabbed him by the collar and trapped him by the wall.

"Saldua, you traitor!" the corporal yelled, "You told us that Estados Unidos is coming to bay! You told us soldiers will attack Intramuros! What happened to Burgos's promises?!"

Intramuros, roughly translated as "within the walls", was the other name of the colonial capital of Manila. It had been the enduring symbol of Spanish power in the Philippines for centuries, the only major colony of Spain in Asia. It was no singular stone fortress like Fort San Felipe, but a magnificent complex of fortresses which was built on the foundations of the ancient kingdoms the Spanish subjugated during their conquest of the Philippines.

"Don't you get it, corporal?" Saldua maniacally laughed, "Nadaya kayo! You've been had!"

He shook Saldua like a dirty rag, "What do you mean, Saldua?! Sumagot ka!"

Suddenly, the corporal heard noises expressing shock and dismay from their own side. Throwing the treacherous soldier hard enough to cause him to roll a few meters away, he then saw what his brothers in arms witnessed. Walking from behind the artillery and the riflemen lined up against them was a most imposing figure. It was the Captain General himself, Rafael Izquierdo. His reputation as an iron handed commander preceded him, with the general being a seasoned veteran of the civil wars in Spain and had once ruled harshly as governor of Puerto Rico. Nobody was more feared in the

Philippines than Izquierdo, who upon assuming office in Spain's only Asian colony wiped out most of the reforms implemented by his predecessors. His presence in the battlefield was intimidating enough to reach even those who guarded the overtaken fort.

The bemedaled general looked at Lamadrid from head to toe, as if he pitied the rebellious sergeant in his tattered uniform and stained sword, although his real opinion of the mutineer may have differed greatly from what observers might think. After all, the Spanish had long regarded Filipinos as a class lower than their own, regardless of prevailing laws and reforms at least in the past century. Izquierdo dared not to differ. With his own sabre in its sheath, Izquierdo motioned for his troops to aim at Lamadrid, yet withheld the ultimate order to fire. It was then when the sergeant met the general in the eyes, his fiery will managing to reach even Izquierdo's callous heart. The loyalist forces, already anxiously waiting for their orders, became even more nervous when Izquierdo slowly approached the mutineer.

"Amado sargento, how much did *La Mano Negra* pay you?" he sternly asked the sergeant, his one hand at the ready to draw his sabre at any time, "Are you taking vengeance because of your pay cuts? Surely you understand the provincia's state of finances."

The general was referring to a suspected international syndicate called the Black Hand which espoused anarchist principles, wreaking the havoc of death even if it meant sacrificing their very lives for the cause. This Izquierdo believed even as intelligence reports indicate how less idealistic causes such as delayed promotions, unpaid wages, and loss of privileges eventually led to the gravity and the coordination of the mutiny. It appeared to him an impossibility unless organized by forces beyond the Filipino's mundane reason.

"El error! I don't know La Mano Negra! I'm not here for such superficial agenda! How different shall we be from animals, if our cause can be placated by temporal pleasures?" Lamadrid courageously replied, concealing with his bravado the waning of his strength, "Hijos del pais! We're children of this country, and we're taking her to a better future! Race, religion, and rank need not matter where equality exists. We fight for liberty and independence of all!"

Izquierdo nodded, "Si, entiendo, that's how it is."

Without any further word, the general slashed upwards, but his sabre clashed with the sergeant's, who abruptly parried the first strike with apparent ease. Seeing an opening on Izquierdo's side, Lamadrid strongly kicked the general, but this was received quite well. Izquierdo did not seem to mind the sergeant's retaliation at all. He then leaped away and shifted his offensive to a variation of stabbing and slashing, Lamadrid keeping up with Izquierdo's speed, but only barely. As he felt his power fading, and Izquierdo gaining the fight's initiative, the sergeant thought he needed to take down the general with a single, final attack.

Swirling to hide the use of an igniter, Lamadrid soon revealed a flaming sword, which blaze spun as it took the momentum from his initial swirl. This final secret sword technique, which he earlier announced to the mutineers in raising their morale, took Izquierdo aback. It was as if hell itself broke loose when he witnessed the inferno from up close. In all his years in the field, there was nothing to compare with this. As the general remained in a state of surprise, the sergeant took the opportunity to wound Izquierdo, putting a piece of the latter's uniform in flames. The general then randomly slashed away, intent on keeping the flaming sword from ever getting near him, as he dashed to escape Lamadrid's fiery wrath.

Suddenly, the thundering sound of gunpowder was heard. It was one of the government soldiers, firing a cannon without orders upon seeing the fear of their captain general. Although his instinct proved quick enough to recognize the threat, his body failed to respond as immediately as he hoped. Izquierdo apparently did enough to push him to the limit. Lamadrid did not have any choice but to deflect the incoming shell with his blazing sabre. As the shell cracked, however, it exploded right in front of the sergeant, blinding him in that instant and blowing him far away from loyalist lines. Seeing what transpired, the general was relieved while the Spanish soldiers loudly cheered. Soon enough, the infantry began rushing to retake the fort.

As for Lamadrid, his blasted frame was caught by one of the mutineers, the corporal who beat Saldua earlier. Even though the sergeant's hearing began to wane as well, he could still recognize the weeping of his troops. Mustering whatever was left of him, Lamadrid slowly raised his sabre and handed it over to the melancholic corporal, whose unintelligible cry was stopped upon hearing his dying superior's words.

"Tu te encargas, cabo," he weakly spoke his last as his eyes lost their shine, "The revolution will not die today. *Hiraya manawari.*"

Izquierdo proved unforgiving in his retaliation against the Cavite Mutiny, rounding up soldiers and civilians alike for the mere suspicion of being involved, invoking even how La Mano Negra, the Black Hand, had supposedly stretched their claws to Philippine shores. It was of no consequence that the mutineers had their own version of what was promised to them. Some of those who got arrested were eventually executed, Saldua himself included in its toll, while others were exiled. This relatively moderate approach, while understood by Izquierdo's peers in the Masonry, were not as appreciated by the religious and the local elites who wanted a bloodier end to the uprising. For them, Izquierdo failed to make a suitable example out of their folly. Nonetheless, it was an episode of oppression and infamy for many Filipinos, including those who were not part of the mutiny. They were reminded of how Spain could be as harsh as any other foreign power for the sake of preserving their sovereignty.

Memories of what became known as the Cavite Munity still flooded the mind of one corporal, Juan Ruiz, who fled the Philippines thereafter. He was the only one of the mutineers to have successfully escaped the captain general's terror hunt, but with this new lease at life he carried a great burden. In a special mission to avenge the Spirit of '72, Ruiz did what he could to fulfill Lamadrid's ultimate wish, the freedom and independence of the Philippines.

After his daring escape, enduring all the colonial security had to offer against survivors like himself, he went for a stint in France to shed all connections with his military past. Why France, one may ask? Just a year prior, the Germans smashed the French spirit after France hindered their prince, Leopold of Hohenzollern, to bid for succeeding the Spanish crown after *La Gloriosa*, the Glorious Revolution in Spain. This loss in what became known as the Franco-Prussian War meant France would unlikely meddle with anything Spanish for the meantime.

However, seeing not much gains for his goals, he subsequently moved to Britain, where he saw the chance to raise necessary funds to jumpstart the new revolution. It was not an entrepreneurial venture, a financial bubble, nor a deceitful scam. Ruiz masterfully robbed 110,000 in pound sterling from the renowned Bank of England, the number 110 being symbolic somehow of the number of years since the British invaded the Philippines. A hefty sum, which brought down to historic lows the bank's reputation and assets. The dishonorable thievery, however, proved only to be the easy part. With police placed all over the world, especially in parts of it directly ruled by Her Majesty, Ruiz found it difficult to smuggle the money out of the country. For a nation which had left its footprint in almost every other country in the world, Britain proved to be a powerful force to reckon with, but he had to take the risk.

What caught his imagination was the stupendous wager of British gentleman Phileas Fogg to circumnavigate the world in 80 days. Quirky it may be in his opinion, even as it involved 20,000 pounds among the primary bettors alone and not counting the wagers made the world over as the journey excited many nations. Yet, it proved a convincingly plausible excuse that Scotland Yard, a name for London's Metropolitan Police, actually suspected Fogg for a while as the bank thief. And so, Ruiz was delighted to see that Fogg failed in his journey. Not only did his return clear him of all accusations, he could most likely try again to travel around the world, and perhaps this time, bring a new assistant that could better help him win another bet.

After all, Fogg did not fail extravagantly. It was a slim margin of a single day as he arrived on Day 81. Then again, as Ruiz, cleverly disguised as a gentleman himself, stalked Fogg's residence in Saville Row without cease, there seemed no indication that the Reform Club member would even dare to venture out of his home. Meanwhile, he had no adequate reason to just barge in Fogg's house and plead to hire him as a valet for yet another around the world trip.

One day, after Christmas, Ruiz spotted a neatly dressed gentleman who came to Fogg's residence, the first time he ever saw any person purposely visiting ever since the famed gambling man's failure. Realizing this as an opportunity to finally reach Fogg, Ruiz did not spare any moment to approach the bifocaled bloke before someone responded to the gate.

"Monsieur," he bowed, feigning as much of a French accent as he could, "My name is John Ruy. Are you in any way related to the resident of this spectacular home?"

"Monsieur Ruy, was it?" the man narrowed his eyes, "What business could you possibly have with Phileas? You're not from Scotland Yard now, are you?"

"Ah, oui, monsieur. Nothing of that sort. I'm interested in his journey around the world! It's of utmost importance. Please, monsieur, can you help me see him?"

Before the gentleman could even reply, a stunning Indian lady clad in an elegant bustle dress and a gleaming jewel hanging on her head opened up the gate. When Ruiz saw the joy in the woman's reception, who had excellent command of the English language, he knew he approached the right person. Ruiz himself, however, appeared quite suspicious in her eyes. Immediately recognizing the atmosphere, the gentleman introduced him with a hearty laugh, preventing her from taking any untoward action against Ruiz.

"It's been a while, eh? By the way, this is my new French valet," he opened, "Mr. John Ruy. John, this is Phileas's wife Aodha."

Picking up on the bloke's ruse, Ruiz bowed, but refrained from holding the lady, "Bonjour, mademoiselle. Charmed to meet you."

"Yes, I understand," her frown turning into a smile, especially after learning that Ruiz was French, "Come in, John, Richard."

"Richard?" the accidental valet muttered.

Hearing what Ruiz thought out loud, he softly responded, "Yes, my good man. The name is Richard Haze, and the favor I'm doing you shall not come cheap."

Ruiz nodded, confident that if Haze would only ask for monetary compensation, he definitely have enough to spare and still not affect the revolutionary financing he planned to take home. Of course, if the person was Fogg's friend, Haze might just be as prosperous a gentleman. Nonetheless, he figured it would be of no significant use considering the possibilities now. The more important goal was to convince Fogg to travel the world again, with him in tow.

The sight of Fogg, however, proved ghastly for both men as they saw the gambler seated by the fireplace. It had only been around a week since he lost his wager, but it was clear that Fogg had deteriorated beyond expectations. He was pale beyond comparison. Never mind going around the world. He might even be unable to tour around his house with the kind of body he had at this moment. His hand even trembled visibly as he placed his tea cup on the table.

With a thin smile, Fogg welcomed his visitors from his seat, "Happy holidays, gentlemen. What brings you to this man's abode? I paid up all my dues, yes?"

Haze rushed to Fogg's side, holding him by the shoulders, "Dear friend, what happened to you?"

When Fogg just stared blankly at him, Aodha walked to her husband's side, replaced his blanket, and explained, "It's no use, Richard. He won't even try my special curry, and I'm his wife."

Loosening his hold of Fogg, Haze asked, "I need to talk to him, Aodha."

"I don't know what to tell you."

She looked at her husband intently, "I always thought had it not been for that wager, I'd have never met my hero Phileas. But after this country milked him dry of his assets, even the company that betted in his favor, he broke down beyond comprehension."

"What about Passepartout?"

Haze referred to the faithful valet who became as famous as his master Fogg. Jean Passepartout, a former member of the French National Guard and once part of a circus, proved to be helpful despite having no significant experience travelling outside Europe. It was also the valet who reminded Fogg to readjust his calendar in accordance to crossing the International Date Line. At the mention of his name, however, Fogg suddenly snapped back to reality.

"Passepartout!" the frail man declared with his hands up, "I'm going to take you back from that Yokohama circus!"

As she patted her husband's back, Aodha sighed, "He doesn't seem to remember now, but after being deprived of his wealth, my darling Phileas fired Passepartout. The Frenchman was willing to work without pay, determined to help his master recover. Alas, Phileas's decision was final. God knows where Passepartout is now."

Haze massaged his forehead, "How could this be? How could one bet ruin a man's life?"

When Fogg calmed his nerves, she turned to Haze, "Why are you here anyway, Richard? You mentioned something about talking to my dear hero?"

Taking out his eyeglasses to clean the lenses, Fogg's friend replied with thrill, "You might not be aware, but the world is still crazy over Phileas's adventure. When big business saw this as an opportunity to boost their sales, they became willing to fund three candidates to try breaking the 80-day barrier. The race begins New Year 1873. The fastest one to travel around the world will win a sum of at least 60,000 pounds, commissions from sponsors and other possible winnings excluded. The losers will go home with nothing."

In this setup, the organizers would produce half of the pot, that is 30,000 pounds, and the contenders would provide the other half of the prize. The sponsoring organizers, however, would not entirely lose money even if they lost the wager because they could earn during the contest period through other means, including a public guesstimate where people could bet not only who would win the wager, but also when the chosen candidate would successfully return. The media coverage to hype the contest was also expected to boost overall sales in the entire duration. The real losers would be the candidates themselves, who would have to pay if they lose.

Aodha's eyes widened, "Richard, you're not telling me that."

"Indeed, I stake my own fortune of 10,000 pounds to go into the fray for the sake of my friend. I'll prove to our colleagues in the Reform Club that Phileas's convictions were not misplaced."

"But Richard," she stretched an arm to him, "surely you'd reconsider, as you saw how a loss would be severely devastating to any man."

Ruiz, who initially lost hope on accompanying Fogg around the world, saw light in Haze's announcement. After being silent the entire time, he boldly seconded the motion.

"Parfait!" Ruiz cheerily said, "I'll be starting preparations for the journey, monsieur."

While puzzled at his pretender valet's enthusiasm, Haze nonetheless received Ruiz's backup well.

"See, Aodha? This is feasible. This is history in the making. It can be done."

It surprised everyone in the room when Fogg once again spoke, but this time, it appeared his delusion had dissipated.

"Richard," Fogg looked at Haze as he weakly touched his friend by the arm, "You'll go around the world?"

With a smile, the sympathetic Haze gave his assurance, "Dear friend, you know me. The money is irrelevant. Pride is not the issue. This is something only you and I will understand, yes?"

The peaceful Fogg nodded, "My spirit will go with you."

"Thank you. Your approval is all I need to push this through."

"Semper reformanda," Fogg said as he squeezed Haze's arm.

"Semper reformanda," Haze replied, holding his friend's cold hand in return for the gesture.

As the two gentlemen left the house, Fogg turned to his wife, yet he did not speak a word. The sudden attention embarrassed Aodha, who despite being his wife had known him for only a number of weeks. He then motioned for her to come closer. She was more than willing to comply.

Reaching for her hand, the gambling man spoke with more vitality than earlier, "Forgive me, Aodha, for being a man defeated. A man who had never travelled outside the country, yet staked everything for a wager to go around the world. I have neglected you. I'm not your hero."

She shook her head while tightening her grasp of his hand, "Phileas, I'll always be here with you."

He blinked, shifting the topic, "That Richard is quite an eccentric gentleman, don't you think so?"

"What do you mean, darling?"

"I thought he's going to ask me for advice about travelling the world," he mused, "Instead, he only asked for my approval. It was like he wanted me to pass a baton, except that baton was not mine to give. He was always intent to carve his own path towards greatness. I wonder how he plans to do it. Three months ago, I was alone. Today, he will have to compete quite fiercely."

She leaned closer, gently hugging his head, "That's what I loved about you. You think of others' sake, even now. You're the epitome of a hero."

After staying like so for a few minutes, Fogg spoke softly, "I'd be happy to try the curry."

Fogg's two visitors, however, were yet to sort out their differences. After all, it was the first time they met, but Ruiz felt he was at a disadvantage because he already implied his purpose to meet Fogg when he voiced an energetic support for Haze's declaration to tour the world. He did not consider how he also had a hint of Haze's intentions as well, assuming it was about to be public knowledge anyway. While walking the busy streets of London, Haze tried to probe his accidental valet further. What was his true motivations in trying to convince Fogg to travel?

"John, was it?" he queried without looking at the man, "Are you genuinely French?"

"Oui, Monsieur Haze. A versatile French worker, if I may say so myself," Ruiz beamed, "I'm willing to travel the world if you permit. I offer every skill I have for your service."

"I understand, but see, Phileas's big mistake was to hire a valet who had about the same travel experience as himself. I was about to contact the valet services for a suitable candidate, but I'm moved by your dedication to accompany Phileas. Dedication always trumps expertise, but–"

"Monsieur, if I may," Ruiz interrupted, "I may not look like it, but I've been to a lot of places. Europe, Asia, Africa. Name it, I've set foot on them."

"Oh," Haze's eyes narrowed, "Why is that so?"

Confident of his fake back story, Ruiz responded, "I'm a migrant worker, monsieur. I work wherever there is work. Assisting people is just one of my tasks. Especially after France's defeat in the war, I figured it safer to be elsewhere than in the midst of my nation's postwar carnage."

A believer of British supremacy in the European continent, Haze somehow understood where Ruiz was coming from, "You're right. How about, say, battle experience?"

"M-monsieur?"

"War. La guerre. The world is not a peaceful place, John. I can't fight too much myself, so I'd like a person who can help defend me when the need arises."

Ruiz bit his lip, thinking of ways to conceal his past as a Filipino soldier, "I, uh, I can handle a sabre."

"Yes, yes. And?"

"A g-gun, too. Rifle or pistol, I guess, it doesn't matter."

"How about bare hands?"

"I can, um, I can manage, monsieur."

Upon hearing these answers, Haze nodded and gave him a piece of paper, "Good show. Report to this address first thing in the morning of December 31. Would that be enough of an allowance for you to arrange what you must?"

The address was written out front, but when he opened the paper, Ruiz also saw 100 pounds. This startled the former soldier. It was an amount sufficient to pay his rent for an entire year. As he was about to thank Haze, however, the gentleman had disappeared from sight. This made Ruiz even more suspicious. He believed his military sense had not waned since the Cavite Mutiny, but here was a person who could easily slip from his presence without much of an effort. Quickly putting the money and the paper inside his pocket, Ruiz walked briskly towards his home, thrilled to realize that his breakthrough was about to come.

Hello World

"Denpou! A telegram for you, daisa."

A Japanese sailor rushed from the communications center of the Yokosuka Naval Arsenal to one of the ships anchored at bay, the ironclad corvette *Ryukansen*. Weighing over 3,000 tons and having a length of 70 meters, it might well qualify as a frigate. The captain of the ship, a beauteous woman of tied black hair named Airi Azuchi, gave the sailor a menacing gaze. This was powerful enough to stop the sailor on his tracks, who was terrified to even take a step further to hand the telegram.

"You call yourself a member of the Nihon Kaigun?!" she bellowed, "You're in the navy now! If you'll hand over an important message, you don't have to yell it to the world, understand?"

Upon snatching the paper from his hand, the sailor gave a sloppy salute and ran as if his very life was threatened. Meanwhile, Azuchi went back to her room at haste, ignoring all the ship's crew who saluted in her presence along the way, before opening the telegram. If it was a telegram addressed to her personally, she had an inkling of who might have sent it and for what purpose was it sent in the first place. The captain only had to confirm this now, and the suspense built up every second she had not yet read the message.

As she settled in her room, seated by the window to have sufficient light for reading, her eyes slowly turned to focus on the telegram, "Risu Tsuringu…"

When she finally absorbed the identity of the sender, Azuchi hugged the paper before continuing.

To the most excellent captain of Ryukansen,

I am writing to you at this moment to confirm that I have acquired a means to bring home the bacon. I am well aware of your love for high quality meat, so it will go the fastest route possible, with a trusted individual undertaking the delivery personally. Please meet at Yokohama on the estimated time of arrival. You cannot miss the next train. Rei-ni, rei-ni, nana-san.

Hoping to see you again, and have an audience with your buried vegetables.

Warm regards, Risu Tsuringu.

The teary-eyed captain attempted to contain her emotions with a soft laugh, "Risu, you really did it, didn't you? How dare you phrase it like you're not the one coming here?"

Then again, who was Risu Tsuringu? As it turned out, it was one of the aliases assumed by Ruiz after he escaped the Philippines. Wary that sending his message of hope to any colony of the European powers might alert the authorities in Britain, and considering his limited connections, he figured his Japanese ties would be the least risky path to relay his initial success since the nation was not dominated by any world power. From there, Filipino immigrants in Japan could take the message back to the Philippines, and help organize ahead of him the continuation of the revolution which they long sought.

At this time, despite policies indicating rising aggressiveness from its more hawkish leaders, Japan was not perceived as a credible threat by any of the European powers, Spain included, as the newly reformed country even courted European and American expertise to build their new military under the Meiji government. More so, Japan itself had the potential to be challenged from within, particularly in relation to the abolition of the domains over a year prior. The local lords, particularly the *tozama daimyo* or outside lords who formed the core of the anti-shogunate movement that helped the Meiji Restoration succeed, were dissatisfied with how the Meiji era was shaping up as the abolition policy disenfranchised them of power and prestige.

In London, Ruiz packed only two bags. One of them had the stash of money from the Bank of England, ingeniously concealed in a metal case which was highly unremarkable on its own, padded with pillows, blankets, even his own clothes, properly folded for that matter. The other literally possessed all the essential stuff he believed would be sufficient for the journey. Hidden within the second bag was a sabre, the one he inherited from Lamadrid, and a pistol, the one he used in the Cavite Mutiny. Both were mementos of the failed uprising, but they were maintained so well, they could still function effectively as weapons despite the passage of time.

Soon enough, he found himself in Haze's home, which proved to be as grand, if not better, than Fogg's own, only because the latter's residence did not seem to be kept well after his loss. Nonetheless, it seemed typical of Victorian architecture. The house itself was symmetrical, with a tall door and an array of wide windows which fitted the intended design perfectly. While apparently built from brick and slate, there were hints of it utilizing steel to reinforce the overall structure. Surrounded by lush gardens, the ornate path to the house was paved with stone. What seemed off from the entire edifice was the absence of a chimney, which made Ruiz wonder how Haze was keeping himself warm during the winter.

"John," Haze greeted him, this time with a jollier mood than before, "You're just in time. Still, no harm with getting here earlier, no?"

"Oui, monsieur," Ruiz bowed, "I apologize for my tardiness."

It was thirty minutes past five in the morning. The sun had not even risen over London, as the city would only see sunlight at around eight in the morning during December.

"No matter," Ruiz's new master waved his hand, "Do welcome yourself in my humble abode. I don't think I have to orient you on valeting, so we'll discuss an important matter first."

The valet quietly followed Haze. Upon entry, the master cranked a lever, causing the house to be illuminated by lightbulbs attached to the walls. This bewildered Ruiz, who had only been acquainted with candles and gas lamps. The bulbs, however, did not contain fire within them, and they shone brightly like a miniature sun without necessarily burning the surroundings.

When Haze saw how Ruiz simply gaped at the sight, he snickered, "I'm sure you're wondering about this old invention. You may call this *bottled light*, but you'll be wiser to call it a lightbulb."

"Old?" the valet widened his eyes, "There's never been any device like this in all of Europe!"

The master lightly tapped Ruiz's back, "You amuse me, John. These bulbs use platinum filaments in them. They've been around since 1840, if I reckon correctly."

"1840! How come it's not being used around the world, monsieur?"

Haze sighed, "Because they're too expensive to replicate. If a cheaper material could be used, I'm sure lightbulbs will take over the world's homes. For now, the entire stock is with me."

It was by this time that Ruiz became more convinced about Haze's wealth. Even Fogg did not have lightbulbs in his home, or even if he did, the gambler might have sold them to pay for his losses.

Following his master, Ruiz then realized he was already in a spacious living room, surrounded by intricately designed chairs and impressive works of art. Yet what would catch the eye easily were the books, maps, notes, pens, compasses, and rulers, among other materials, littered over a large table in the middle. Upon taking a seat, Haze motioned his new valet to take be seated opposite him. Ruiz immediately complied.

With a hand on his chin, the master asked, "Take a look at this. You've been travelling around, John. Your opinion would be helpful in my last-minute planning."

"What do you mean, monsieur?" the startled Ruiz almost fell from his seat, "Why would a gentleman as yourself ponder on the word of a servant? Your word is law in our relationship."

Haze frowned, "Slavery has been abolished in most of the world now. All people are equal. Put simply, we're peers. Only there are people who went on ahead, and others who lagged behind, but that doesn't mean superiority. It's all a matter of being at the right time."

"I, I understand," the valet was awed at Haze's progressive thinking, realizing as well how the master continually regarded him with his first name.

At first glance, contrasts may be seen in the master's personal beliefs. How could a man who saw Britain as ahead in this world be a champion of human rights and equal opportunity? Upon closer examination, however, his confidence of British leadership of the world was founded only on his nationalism. In foresight, Haze believed Britain should take efforts to remain ahead, for progress would be no monopoly of any one nation or race. There would be no chance for the country to regain industrial supremacy with American and European economies overtaking British production, but Britain could create a new era beyond the factory, and lead the way.

One demonstration of the world's progress as a whole was Fogg's circumnavigation. It was made possible because the rest of the world was catching up well enough to even facilitate the journey. One could only shudder imagining if Fogg was detained in a place where no viable means of transport was available. Tomorrow, more would attempt to break his record, but today, Haze had a more pressing matter to resolve than worrying about the next century.

"Good," the master nodded as he cleared some of the materials to reveal a marked map, "Back to the task. I traced Phileas's journey, and he had nine major stops. Calais in France, Brindisi in Italy, Suez in Egypt, Bombay and Calcutta in India, Hong Kong in China, Yokohama in Japan, San Francisco and New York in America. But he's wrong to trust the Queen's overseas holdings to complete his journey. In fact, most of his delays were in British territories, particularly India and Hong Kong. He may have found love, yes, but he lost his fortune, too."

When Ruiz saw how Fogg's route went nowhere near the Philippines, he found a chance to influence his new master to take a path that would bring him back home, "You're certainly right, monsieur. But why do you think that is?"

Haze slammed the table, much to the valet's surprise, "Because they suspected Phileas of robbing the Bank of England, that's what!"

Upon hearing these words, sweat began to form on Ruiz's body. The temperature was quite cold in their room despite the house heating system, which was actually comprised of fans pulling the air out, warming the place in the process. This explained the lack of chimneys in Haze's home. At least, the reported low temperature at this time was cold enough to freeze water, but apparently insufficient to keep the valet from sweating.

As Ruiz subtly averted looking at Haze, the master nonetheless continued in voicing his grudge, "And I suspect, highly for a fact, that Scotland Yard would try to delay my journey as well. With the bank thief still missing, even our colleagues in the Reform Club, even that peasant of a Chancellor who is now Prime Minister, would try to put the blame on anyone who looked like flowing with silk and money."

The Bank of England, while established as a private bank, had become a *lender of last resort* during the Panic of 1866, a function usually performed by a central bank. This raised public perception that the Chancellor of the Exchequer, the head of Her Majesty's Treasury, had intentionally tied the renowned bank to the government. Trouble with the Bank of England, therefore, would likely find its way to the top of British governance.

"Monsieur…," the valet tried to calm Haze, but found no suitable words to appease his master.

"To sum, I intend to avoid all British territories. My proposed path is Paris, Hamburg, Berlin, Frankfurt, Warsaw, Moscow, Vladivostok. Two weeks should be enough if we don't stop for anything else. From there, I have a number of options to take. What do you suggest, John?"

Ruiz gulped, thinking that it might blow his cover if he suggested something out of line with his master's proposal. There were a number of routes which overlapped in Haze's map, but there was a particular path that caught his interest. He traced this with his finger before speaking.

"If I may, monsieur. This seems good to me. Vladivostok, Busan, Yokohama, Manila, Hawaii, Acapulco, Havana, Azores, London."

Haze studied each of the key points mentioned, "I see. You mean to avoid the British world altogether. America, too. This is aligned with what I seek to do. But my concern is this."

He pointed at Manila, "This feels like a waste of travel time to me. It would take a week to reach Manila from Yokohama. What do you think stops us from going straight to Acapulco?"

The valet was at a loss. He may be a soldier with a good sense of geography, but there was no logical comeback to Haze's comprehension. It would take at least 24 days to travel from Yokohama to Acapulco, but that would be extended by a week if they make the detour through Manila. If the race was not intended to merely to finish the journey in 80 days, but to complete it earlier than the other competitors, Haze could not afford to take any inefficient detours. Then again, if he chose to cross through America, would have he been faster? Using the figures in his master's map, Ruiz mentally calculated at haste to try persuading Haze.

"Um, the southern waters would warm us after enduring the Siberian taiga?"

Haze shook his head, "I appreciate your attention, but I'm willing to stake my well-being if it meant taking the lead in this race."

With a forced smile, Ruiz gave his approval, "Oui, monsieur. Yokohama it is. I'll note it down."

His mind, however, screamed in desperation as Haze's decision meant he would not be able to bring the money personally to the Philippines and launch the revolution with his countrymen. The Filipino immigrants in Japan would be helpful at this juncture, but even he doubted their resolve to complete the mission. He even thought they might keep the money for themselves, which he hoped against. Ultimately, he believed he was tasked by the late Lamadrid himself to pursue the freedom of their people. Nonetheless, without Haze's journey, he might not be able to leave Britain at all, and his robbery would be naught.

"Thank you, John," Haze shook his hand, "You proved in this meeting that you have enough geographic experience to travel the world with me."

The visibly confused Ruiz queried, "Monsieur, you don't mean this was another test?"

"You got it," the master pointed at him, "But actually, I'm also contemplating all the options I have. Your suggestion gave me the assurance that I'm going in the right direction."

"Uh, I, well, thank you, I guess?"

Writing down on his notebook as well, Haze smirked, "Barring any delays, we can return in 70 days. We may even reach London earlier, if a blessing comes our way."

"Seventy!" Ruiz exclaimed, thinking that it would have been wise to have given Captain Azuchi an earlier date, "That's even faster than what the papers say!"

"They will manipulate the numbers, keeping the public guessing in a betting game that already makes them money regardless of who the winner would be," the master nodded, "Yes, an acceptable outcome, but we have to make haste. As soon as the opening ceremony ends tomorrow, we'll go for the first ship to Paris on a steam bus."

"Monsieur," the valet protested, "Didn't the government ban the use of any automated vehicle to go over 6 kilometers an hour?"

Ruiz was referring to the Red Flag Act, which limited the speed of all road locomotives. With this speed limit, it was ensured that motorized vehicles would only go slightly faster than walking. The red flag, meanwhile, was used by the person assisting the vehicle to signal stoppage when deemed necessary.

"A likely story," Haze laughed, "I've already hired a driver to take us. At 40 kilometers per hour, we'll be at Dover in two hours flat. You can't do that with any horse-driven carriage."

"But monsieur!"

"John, I don't care if they flag me red because of this. We take every innovation we get at reasonable prices we can, because who else will support progress than ourselves?"

The two gentlemen would then proceed to prepare everything for their lengthy journey around the world. Haze himself did not seem to be a man who needed a lot of baggage. He was taking two bags himself, but as to how much the Reform Club member would be willing to spend for this race, it was yet beyond Ruiz. He could only speculate, as his master the next morning gave him a preliminary fund of 2,000 pounds before they proceeded to the ceremony. A hefty sum, as it was already a fifth of what Haze wagered to beat Fogg's record.

Instead of the Reform Club, which saw Fogg's wager develop, the venue was the grandiose Hyde Park, host of the 1851 Great Exhibition, an exposition of British strength and prosperity relative to the world, where they found themselves in the midst of some 60,000 people. If there was a pound taken from every person in the venue, the organizers would have already recouped their expenses without resorting to taking the competitors' money. Still, businessmen saw no harm in earning just as well in the opening.

Despite arriving early, however, Haze found himself last in the stage of honor, with his competitors already seated proudly. It was ten in the morning. With their judgmental eyes, the two women in working dresses and sturdy overcoats saw him as a bumbling gentleman who misunderstood the challenge he entered. In truth, little was known to the public about Haze, while the other candidates were quite famous, and the speaker pumping up the crowd did not spare words in describing the highly touted contenders for international fame and fortune.

First to be called was the American writer and entrepreneur Jane Plain, who in contrast to her name did not appear anywhere near plain. Her appearance was so outstanding, she could cut her hair and wear men's clothing, yet still be recognized as a gorgeous woman. She spoke like a persuasive stateswoman with unparalleled oratorical skills. Indeed, she was being considered as potential candidate for governor or senator in her home state in the coming elections. The paragon of the

American Dream, Plain was a self-made businesswoman who founded her enterprise in shoes. Noticing the shortage of quality footwear, Plain took advantage of mass production techniques and the introduction of cheap material to launch her own brand called Plain Shoes. At affordable prices, coupled with branding that appealed to the public, although it was merely wordplay of her name, Plain Shoes allowed her to branch out and expand her empire in other ventures, the press included. After all, it would be a good platform for her to be able to advertise her products in a widely circulated medium. Not only would her own publication sponsor her journey, she also had allies in sister media companies in Europe and Asia.

The second to be called was also as distinguished a personality as Plain. Austrian singer and banker Minerva Rausch, however, did not come from humble beginnings as her American rival. The scion of a banking family, Rausch enjoyed the perquisites of being a Freiin, a baroness by virtue of being a baron's daughter, to jumpstart her singing career. Compounded by her talent, her success spread like fire throughout Europe, where she became known as the Singing Princess, even though she was no princess. This was not to say it was a rose garden for Rausch, for her family initially rejected her passion for singing and dismissed it as nothing more than an aimless hobby, especially as she began her career with tours around the Austrian Empire which targeted both city and countryside alike. This ostracization influenced her early compositions.

Nonetheless, her voice proved to be a turning point for the family's banking business as well, with

Rausch banks featuring so-called *singing stations* which became a hit with investors and depositors. With the development of sound transmitters in the 1860s, Rausch devised a system to make her songs heard within a certain coverage area of their branches through connecting all the transmitters in their bank branches to a central studio, where she would sing for a fixed time period for all to hear. However, if people would seek to avail of this performance, they would have to conduct a transaction in any bank branch covered. For Rausch's well-being, meanwhile, her family had also financed the development of recording systems to accompany the transmission systems they already laid. This way, she would not have to sing live from a studio every time. The music quality may leave much to be desired for the technology of this time, but people still enjoyed Rausch's songs. And thus, after a quick speech which banked more on her popularity than anything else, the dazzling singer gave the Hyde Park audience a powerful and unforgettable show featuring her latest song. With sister banks around the world, Rausch virtually had unlimited credit at her disposal to help facilitate her world tour.

The crowd quieted down when it was Haze's turn to be introduced. Even the speaker tried to contain his low expectations for the third contender to break Fogg's record. Other than his membership in the Reform Club, there was nothing remarkable about his public profile. Even his credentials as a member of such a high-level gentlemen's club the audience doubted. They wondered how a person such as he could somehow be considered a peer of the Prime Minister, the Governor of the Bank of England, and even the now famous globetrotter Phileas

Fogg. His message to the people outlining what he brought to the table did not seem to leave a mark either. Haze's ideals of responsible British leadership of the world and helping the nations prosper fell on deaf ears. For those who did listen, he appeared an out-of-touch reformist who represented not the new era he advocated, but futurist lunacy that might not even pass as a novelty of a trend. This caused some in the audience to spread malicious stories about him while Haze was still barnstorming on the stage. His appeal as a contender reminded of the proponents of the Second Reform Act, which doubled the number of eligible voters in Britain. They thought this would help them win the election, but the enlarged electorate gave them an even worse defeat in the polls in 1868 as compared to the last one conducted prior to the Reform Act, in 1865. Haze would not even qualify as a dark horse, but he might well be considered a black sheep. If the largely unknown gentleman hoped his participation in the contest would improve his standing in history, almost everyone in Hyde Park disagreed. All except one, his own valet Juan Ruiz.

One part of his master's discussion struck him – the equity of peoples and the liberty of the colonies. Perhaps nobody even bothered to heckle him at that point, for who would survive speaking against the expansionist desire of the largest empire in the world? Yet when Haze talked about the potential of the colonized to leap forward, chart their own destinies, and take their place in the world, Ruiz was mesmerized. Not since the failed promises of the Cavite Mutiny was the former soldier enthralled. It was mighty similar to their private chat about the fast and the slow. The world powers may have had a head start with their industrial capacity, but innovation could allow less developed economies to catch up with lightning speed, or even lead. This made Ruiz ponder if Fogg, being his friend, also espoused the same ideals.

The speaker, noticing the audience's lack of attention, impolitely cut short Haze's speech and went on to explain the mechanics of this highly anticipated race around the world.

"Hello world! Eighty days, three candidates, one prize," he announced like a thrilled salesman, "Who do you think will beat Phileas Fogg's record of travelling the world?"

As the audience yelled their own preferences, the speaker motioned for calm before continuing, "The world is vast, but globalization has shrunk it. This is how it will unfold. The earliest to reach the entrance of Hyde Park will win, but they have to prove their key destinations with corresponding documentation in chronological order, so no fake passports. Photographs are allowed as evidence, but they are not necessary nor primary. We know how studios nowadays can duplicate our surroundings. Telegrams for updates are also allowed, but again, this is secondary. We have correspondents around the world to do the same job, so our challengers will not have to sweat it. We will measure the race down to the last second, so make your bets. Remember, the more slots you buy, the more chances of winning. The race begins... now!"

Fail Early

"I beg your pardon? What do you mean we missed the ship to Paris?"

Despite his apparent anger about the situation, Haze maintained his composure. If one did not know him personally, he might even come across as someone caressing. Unlike Fogg's night departure, this new attempt to tour the world in 80 days began at one in the afternoon. Haze's distrust of British systems, however, made him skip the train to Dover and went along with the planned steam bus ride to start the journey. Fortunately, it went better than expected, the steam bus even reaching a top speed of 60 kilometers per hour. This was still slower than what a train could achieve at its top velocity, but Haze would not expect safety would be jeopardized for the sake of haste. The debacle they met at Dover derailed all planning right from the start, with the ship bound for Paris leaving early.

"Monsieur, forgive me," Ruiz profusely apologized, "I made sure the timetables we had were updated when we left. I'm sorry the sudden change was beyond me."

"No matter," the master strongly tapped his cane once, "What's the first ship we can get on?"

Surveying the harbor's schedule in horror, Ruiz could only reply, "Monsieur, all ships to France have been rescheduled. We can't board any in the next four hours!"

Clenching the fist holding his cane, Haze grinned, "So that's how we play the game, yes?"

He quickly wrote on his notebook, peeled the page, and gave it to Ruiz, "Find me this ship quickly. I'm sure it's still at port around this time."

Taking his bags with him, the valet rushed to look for the indicated vessel. After asking around, he immediately found a small steel ship which did not seem to be carrying passengers. Approaching one of the crew unloading boxes into the ship, it was confirmed that he got to the correct ship. However, what the sailor said next discouraged him.

"I don't know why you're here, mate," he carelessly spoke his thoughts, "She's scheduled to be scuttled, if that's what you want to know."

"What?! That's impossible!" the stupefied Ruiz could not hide his emotions, "Surely you can make a favor for my master, Richard Haze!"

"Did you say Haze?" asked a bulky man with a red beard from the deck, "That crazy son of a—"

"Yes, monsieur," the valet interrupted, "But may I know who you are?"

"Why, I'm the captain, that's who!" he exclaimed, "And by the looks of it, good old Haze needs my help again! Tell him to come over here, then we'll talk about it, eh?"

Thinking that the captain may change his mind about meeting his master if he lingered any longer, Ruiz went back to Haze at the soonest. When they reached the ship, however, the bearded man welcomed Haze with a lariat, which appeared to have caught the gentleman off guard. This sent the master tumbling backwards as the captain guffawed.

"Monsieur!" Ruiz ran towards Haze, frightened of his condition after that attack, "Are you well?"

Grasping his cane to stand, the master startled his valet when he laughed, "Rossa, you sneak!"

It confounded him more when he saw Haze and the captain shaking hands, as if a horrifying event had not transpired between them.

"Good work, John," the master motioned for the valet to take the bags as he made an introduction, "This is Captain Rossa, and the love of his life, Wenn Im August."

When Haze referred to the ship, it was at this moment when Ruiz realized what it was. Wenn Im August was a cargo ship. However, due to its size, the captain lamented that her service was about to be terminated. Speed was not a problem, as it could go as fast as 40 kilometers per hour on a full load, a match for any large cargo ship in the sea, but operators did not appreciate how it could only carry so much. Wenn Im August would pale in comparison with Ryukansen.

"But Rossa," Haze pleaded, trying to pull the friendship card on him, "maybe you can still give her one more voyage. As you can see, I took the wager to travel the world, but my opponents have aced me to it. They rescheduled all trips to France."

With his arms crossed, Rossa frowned, "What's in it for me, Haze, huh? I won't risk getting sunk for your sake. Nah, never again."

"She's going to sink either way, my friend," the master reasoned, "Wouldn't you want your ship to be part of this grand tour of the world?"

The captain scratched his head, "What's with this sense of history and prestige, mate? Can it feed me and my starving crew, eh? We've got nowhere to go after my love's gone for good."

With his hand, Haze motioned for his valet to present a suitable offering. However, when Ruiz handed over 200 pounds, the captain was aghast.

Appalled, the master shot a sharp look at the puzzled valet, "Are you thinking, John? We're persuading the good captain to flout the laws of the sea for us, and you're giving him spare change?"

He then turned to his friend, who was still reeling from the thought of being given a few hundred pounds for his ship's final trip, "Forgive me. See, he's new around here. How does a thousand pounds sound to you, Rossa?"

Ruiz was about to protest, but the captain's firm acceptance of the deal overshadowed everything else that could be pointed out concerning the seemingly extravagant expense. While this delighted the master, who immediately ordered his valet to load their bags in the ship, Ruiz was deep in thought even as his body operated like a machine attending to Haze's demands. It was not as if 200 pounds was a small figure. One could already obtain an economy class ticket to the United States with 20 pounds. Thus, it baffled him, especially since he believed his master had far less financing than the two other candidates. The thought bothered him so much, he largely missed the conversation between the captain and his master as Wenn Im August sailed.

"I never thought of you as a gambler, Haze," the calmer Rossa said, "Why take this wager?"

Haze grinned, "Is it just you've been too cautious since we almost sunk with Sekunden in Moll back in '61?"

As if hearing a forbidden word, the captain clutched to his chest, "You say it like a casual affair!"

"I'll answer you, Rossa, only because we might never see each other again after this."

"Don't put it like that, eh. With the money you gave me, I can probably keep working in Dover. I'd still have enough to bet on your success."

The gentleman put a hand on the bearded captain's shoulder as they looked at the horizon, "Touring the world is not a matter of novelty. It is an exposition of our humanity and our morality. If I lay down my life for my principles, I regret nothing."

"You're kidding," the laughing Rossa placed an arm behind Haze's head, "This ain't more than a rich man's sport, mate. And you know better."

After a good night's rest, Ruiz woke up early in the morning to prepare their things and stretch his legs. When he peered from the window, however, he found that they were still at sea. Quietly treading the room, the valet quickly proceeded to the bridge, where he saw Rossa with some of the crew. Without regard for the apparent seriousness of the work they were doing, Ruiz confronted the captain, hiding none of his disappointment that was partly attributable to the sum of money Haze provided for the purpose.

"Monsieur capitaine," Ruiz opened, "The trip to France won't take more than a few hours. It's been 16 hours, and we're still at sea!"

Rossa frowned as he tried to intimidate the valet with his size, "John Ruy, was it? The fool who tried to buy my love's last voyage with 200 pounds! Were you even listening yesterday, or did your pompous blunder stuff your ears to the brim?"

The valet raised an eyebrow, "Would you care to elaborate?"

The captain sighed so loud, it almost sounded like the hissing of a ship, "We're not going to France. Don't you remember? Haze suspects you are personae non grata there."

"Then where are we going?"

"See for yourself," Rossa motioned his hand to the window, "Even an idiot like you can understand with the eyes, eh."

As the fog cleared, the place they were about to arrive at became visible. It appeared to be a bustling town cut by a river. Factories and similar industrial edifices towered all over, they almost filled the entire horizon. There were also ships at the harbor, but it was immediately recognizable that many of them were not commercial vessels. Those were military and supply ships, with innumerable number of soldiers guarding in their vicinity.

"This isn't France," Ruiz muttered.

"Of course, it ain't!" the captain chuckled, "Welcome to Deutsches Kaiserreich, the German Empire. I've to get a special permit just to see this going, eh. Be thankful, you ingrate!"

As they bade their goodbye to the captain and his soon-to-be scuttled ship, the two travelers realized they were in the town of Kiel. Located in the northern sector of the empire, the port town was nearer to Denmark than to Berlin. While it had been less than a decade since Kiel transferred to German rule, however, the town had been transformed into a naval base at a spectacular pace. Then again, the remarkable growth of the formerly Danish town did not attract Haze's attention, much to Ruiz's surprise. For someone who always talked about progress, the imperial wedge that propelled Kiel's prosperity seemed of little consequence to the British gentleman. Haze, however, had every reason to ignore imperial investments in their newly-acquired territory, more so because it was abetted by British assistance. In his mind, German innovation may be a potent threat to British leadership of the world, an encompassing statement the Germans subtly demonstrated in their victory over the similarly imperialist French two years earlier. He believed his own people were unknowingly helping the creation of this very threat without taking significant steps towards keeping up the pace.

After having his passport and papers checked without a hitch by the consulate, Haze was only relieved to know that Kiel was connected recently to Berlin by rail. Before boarding the train, Haze saw a female beggar asking for alms in German. While he did not seem to fully comprehend what she was saying, the British gentleman quickly took out 20 pounds and gave it to her. As Ruiz peered on the window to see what the beggar would do, he was glad to see her leaving the station with leaps of joy. The valet's impression of his master had improved after this affair.

Within 24 hours, they have travelled over a thousand kilometers from London to the German capital. Even though it was the largest city in the entire empire, Haze appeared more disinterested with the place than he was with Kiel, much to Ruiz's dismay. It was not because the valet wanted to see the sights such as the 82-year-old Brandenburg Gate, but he sought a closer look at the nation which humiliated the French and the Austrians in the field. The center of German power, Berlin was one of the world's greatest cities, and if one would be impressed by Kiel's transformation, the pace at Berlin was even more spectacular. When one would think there was no more space in the city, construction sites left and right continue to emerge like mushrooms. Traffic seemed to flow quite smoothly even while seas of crowds and vehicles flooded Berlin's paved thoroughfares. Alas, taking lessons was least in the priorities of his master. It seemed he already had a fixed impression about the newly forged empire. Was it because he had been in Germany before? It was beyond Ruiz if the gentleman had more travel experience than his friend Fogg, but he had to shelve his thoughts as he met his master's demands.

Firm on taking the immediate next train to Warsaw, Haze then wanted to be left undisturbed in his train cabin, which he took as an opportunity to rest. At its operating speed, it would take around eight hours before they reach the frontier city of the Russian Empire. The Duchy of Warsaw was an independent state during the Napoleonic Wars, albeit behaving more as a client to Napoleon Bonaparte's France than a sovereign nation. After Napoleon's defeat, however, Warsaw came under Russian control as a result of the Congress of Vienna in 1815, the area becoming known as Russian Poland. While it had since been elevated by name from a duchy to a kingdom, the Polish knew better their position in the postwar order. Past were the days of *King* Jadwiga and the *Black Knight* Zawisza. The people of Warsaw could only hope that one day, an independent Poland would emerge, but at the moment, even the empire they were part of was not immune to the wave of reforms swamping the continent.

As Ruiz shamelessly overheard the talk of the passengers in the train, much had been said about the 1861 emancipation of the serfs across the empire, the lifting of censorship, and the opening of local elections, but what worried more the valet was the discussion about Russia's secret police. After the failed assassination attempt against the tsar, the Russian head of state, its organization was formed in St. Petersburg in 1866. The Okhrannoye Otdeleniye or the Department for Protecting Order eventually became an omnipresent institution in the empire.

Among other nationalities, the British had earned the ire of the Russian government when Britain joined France in supporting the Ottoman Empire over Crimea in 1853. More so, the British looked down on Russia as a sort of backwater of the European continent, perhaps forgetting that the empire had not lagged behind the industrial race. It would be easy to pin charges on a British gentleman such as Haze, who was entering Russian territory with nothing more than an excuse of going around the world. In light of his master's potential disadvantage, the valet became eager to protect him at all costs. Approaching what seemed to be a respectable Russian gentleman who he heard speaking ample English and making good music, Ruiz sought to know more.

"Buenos dias, señor. Your mastery of the piano is heavenly," he introduced, shedding his French cover for this conversation, "My name is Juan Pasaporte. This is my first time in the Russian Empire. I was hoping a good señor like yourself could help me understand the country better?"

Motioning his hand to invite Ruiz to seat opposite him, the Russian gentleman clad in an evening jacket gave a jovial reply, "Mr. Pasaporte, a pleasure to meet a fellow passenger, and an enthusiast of modern music. The name's Tulevik. Please do excuse my English. For someone who doesn't look like native to the language, I say, your diction is quite good."

"You flatter me, señor. If I may, I heard rumblings of left-leaning revolutionaries pouring into Russia. Do you think it would impede my travel to, say, Moscow?"

Tulevik's smile evaporated when he heard the Russian capital, "What do you plan to do in Moskva? There's nothing to see there for a Spaniard as yourself."

Desperately searching for a plausible explanation, the valet was only able to say, "The conservatory! Si, si, I seek to enter the Imperial Conservatory."

After taking a sip of wine, the Russian averted his eyes from Ruiz to gaze at the bleak landscape, "Vienna would have been a better choice in my opinion."

The Austrian capital of Vienna was known as the City of Music because of its reputation as a creative hub for musicians and composers from all over the world.

"What can I say?" Ruiz shrugged.

"I believe you," Tulevik said upon returning his look at the valet, "It's just that I won't recommend a foreigner as yourself to stay too long in that nightmare of a city."

Ruiz gulped, his relief of Tulevik believing his story replaced by fear of what Russia might have in store, "S-señor, where are you getting at?"

In a softer voice, the musician leaned to respond, "You heard correctly of leftist activity in Russia. In fact, their near success in taking out the tsar created a reactionary government that stifled everything. Even music, mind you. I'm only returning to Estonia to arrange my final requirements to move to Germany. They seemed to be friendly with the Germans lately, I doubt they will attempt to block my transfer of citizenship."

The valet's eyes widened, "Señor Tulevik, is this country deep in trouble?"

"The Polish alone launched two great rebellions in the past decade. Don't believe the façade of Russian industry and the tsar's emancipation. For the sake of national development, it was the colonized such as the Polish and the Estonians who carried most of the burden."

"But my master is British. Do you think he will be safe in Russia?"

This time, it was the musician's turn to be startled, "You have a master?"

Realizing his blunder, Ruiz tried to reconcile his earlier back story, "My mentor, I mean. He also wants to visit me in the conservatory one of these days."

"Sometimes the English language mystifies me," Tulevik shook his head, "Still, I'm not the best judge of his character. If the Department can't find anything to raise their suspicions, I'm quite certain they will leave him unharmed. Russia has shaky relations with Britain. I doubt they'll start a diplomatic incident over a musician, da?"

The valet laughed nervously, "Si, señor. I believe so, too."

After a less serious conversation and a few rounds of playing with dominoes, Ruiz called it a day and upon leaving, he thought that he made a good acquaintance with the musician. When he returned to their cabin, the refreshed Haze seemed interested to know what his valet had been up to. Ruiz conveniently left out the details where he had to invent his back story, emphasizing instead Tulevik's music, Moscow's winter weather, and rumors about revolutionaries. As he listened, the master unknowingly nodded off once more, making Ruiz uncertain which information he had to repeat for him later on. When the train arrived earlier than expected, however, it did not seem he had to worry about that.

With the formalities of documentary checks taken care of easily, Haze became more occupied with finding the train to Moscow. Despite Warsaw's size, it did not prove difficult. What irritated the gentleman, however, was the bureaucratic process. Apparently, it was not sufficient to have your papers checked in the consulate. The feared secret police, clad in uniform which distinguished them from train officials, were also taking their time inspecting at the rail station itself, devouring whatever time was saved from the early arrival of the Berlin train. Sensing his master's agitation, Ruiz prayed that Haze would keep his calm in the midst of the cold Polish climate. If he caused a scene, it might impede the journey further.

"Alright, that's it!" the Russian officer announced as the horns signaled preparation for departure, "We've reached the train's quota. You have to wait until tomorrow for the next trip."

While the officer's English was less comprehensible than that of the musician's, what he said was clear enough to register what just occurred. Ruiz's hopes were dashed with that pronouncement, and the inevitable had come to pass.

Haze rushed to the officer and grabbed him by the arm, "Nyet, I won't accept this! My journey won't be delayed here! Clearly there's a mistake and you have to rectify it immediately!"

"Guzno!" the officer yelled as he struggled to break free from the gentleman's grasp.

Nine other Russian officers immediately went to help, but there was no stopping Haze from attacking them all on his own, causing the train to halt its engine until the issue was resolved. This sudden display of outrage baffled Ruiz, who had never seen his master lose composure even once since they met in December. Haze did not even care less about losing his glasses, which broke in the midst of the fighting. He was divided on whether to come to his master's aid, as a valet may be expected to do so, or allow the authorities to curb his temper, as an innocent traveler who sought to keep himself away from trouble. As if a person possessed, the gentleman appeared somehow capable of taking on an entire squad of the secret police. Soon enough, a higher ranked officer, apparently a major judging from his epaulette, emerged with a gun in hand. This cleared up all conditions for Ruiz to jump in front of the Russian major.

"Sir, please," the valet appealed profusely, "My master and I only wanted to board the train to Moscow at the soonest possible. We're under the impression we can ride today because tickets were sold to us. We bought first class tickets, but the officers said there are no more seats."

The major looked at Ruiz for a while, and then placed his gun in a holster before shouting, "Smirno!"

The Russian secret police, shocked at the presence of a ranking officer, scrambled to stand in attention, almost dropping Haze on the platform.

As the master straightened his coat and asked his valet for another pair of eyeglasses, he firmly approached the major, "Are you going to arrest me, too? I'm a gentleman!"

"Yes, sir," Ruiz seconded, determined at concealing his French accent as he was aware of Russian apprehensions of France, "My master is beyond reproach."

"Let me see your papers then," the major replied after listening to what the two have to say.

Upon setting his eyes on the documents, the ranking officer sternly asked, "You're British, but you came from Berlin?"

"We passed through it, yes," Haze coolly responded.

"What is your purpose in Moskva?"

"None of your business."

The major frowned, "I'm afraid it is part of my business, Mr. Haze. Would you mind a check on your baggage as well?"

When Haze nodded, anxiety built up for Ruiz. What he believed was the immunity of a gentleman seemed to have faded upon entering the Russian Empire. He searched for a plausible excuse to keep the stash of money from being found out as he assisted the officers in searching.

"Sirs," the valet then attempted to divert their attention before they got to the last bag, "Would you be so kind to skip the final bag? I just fixed it, and now it's too packed, the contents may burst if we open it."

The major scoffed, "All the better. Open it."

Shoving Ruiz aside, they opened the last bag, and as the valet predicted, clothes and souvenirs sprang like rubber, leaving the pudgy pillows inside.

"Alright, I believe you!" the Russian bellowed as he shielded his face from the springing action, "You're good to go! But arrange first all these before you board!"

He may be quietly picking up his things, but the valet was internally relieved that they did not insist on a more stringent search. More importantly, they would be able to board the last train off Warsaw, albeit the trip itself was ultimately delayed because of Haze's assault. It was fortunate that they did not face charges, or worse imprisoned. This might permanently affect their overall chances of winning the wager. The self-congratulations, however, seemed too early. The major immediately proceeded to the telegraph station to send a message to Moscow.

"To the Department," he dictated to the encoder in Russian, "Suspicious British gentleman Richard Haze and valet John Ruy crossed through Berlin, arriving in Moskva. ETA 20 hours. Surveillance is strongly recommended. Arrest if necessary."

The media, meanwhile, were quick to pick up the incident in Warsaw despite the operations of the secret police. Back in Britain, the people woke up to startling news on the third day of the race around the world. Plain was crossing the Atlantic aboard the British ship Victoria, which name she believed was fitting to start her soon-to-be triumphant voyage. Rausch was back in her homeland Austria, where she was received as a heroine even as her journey had only just begun. Utilizing the speed of the

Orient Express thus far, which lines reached as far as the Ottoman Empire, she believed her choice of starting with a land route held the advantage over Plain. Unbeknownst to them at the time, however, an even bigger news event made betting stations open at fever pitch with frenzied crowds forming out of nowhere to buy their slots.

Haze taking on the Russian secret police in the open made headlines, raising patriotic spirits as the British still remember their experience with battling Russia during the Crimean War, which saw the rise of immortalized figures such as Florence Nightingale. His dash to Moscow, while relegated as secondary in the coverage, was not left missed by spectators. Some even commented how he reached the heart of Russia faster than Napoleon ever did. For the first time, the British gentleman became recognized as a viable competitor, if not only because his feat excited the press and the public. Not all, however, were jubilant over Haze's progress.

The British government for instance, while some among them were his fellow Reform Club members, stressed over the gentleman's apparent choice to travel across Russia. With the robber of the Bank of England still at large, they saw another potential security issue erupting if they fail to protect a bona fide British citizen, even as he was in foreign soil. The unstable relations with Russia, however, limited whatever options they had in place. There were also concerns about Haze's background, which seemed to run counter against his recent actions in Warsaw.

How could a Reform Club member such as he had acted so rashly? Did he consciously intend to humiliate the British who expressed no confidence over his chances? Was he a closet anarchist who held authorities in contempt and had demonstrated his leanings as soon as he left the country? At the least, they were not alone in trying to figure out the gentleman's motives. His own valet Ruiz was also intrigued, but for the entire trip to Moscow, he found no good opportunity to open up on the topic. With his master wishing to be left undisturbed, his attention shifted to crossing the Russian Empire without any further incidents. The revolution funds were near in being found out, but he had to maintain their secret all throughout.

Power Failure

"My apologies, but the next Trans-Siberian train will not be available in three days."

Frustration mounted between Ruiz and the train employee in the ticket booth. The valet worried what his master would do if he realized their journey would be stuck in Moscow for a while, especially as the gentleman had given up his privilege to rest in a decent room for three straight days in order to keep the pace. The 9,300-kilometer line reportedly conducted trips at least thrice a week, and at best every day, baffling Ruiz about the sudden unavailability of any trains. The Russian, however, proved quite adamant, citing how only military personnel were allowed to take the trains which operated daily. This coincided with news about emancipated peasants taking arms to disrupt the Siberian economy, thus prompting the Russian government to suppress such subversive elements, but the valet was unconvinced.

"Is there a problem, John?" the master's sudden question sent chills to Ruiz's spine.

When he saw the employee shaking his head, Haze did not need the valet's answer to realize the situation. The expected outburst, however, did not come. Instead, the gentleman calmly ordered him to take their bags and leave the station. It increased the anxiety Ruiz had, for his master became even more unpredictable at this juncture. His suspicions were heightened when he saw they were not heading to any hotel or temporary accommodation in Moscow. Hailing a carriage, Haze spoke what sounded like Russian to the coachman, which to the valet's surprise did not seem any further word to elaborate. Soon enough, they were exiting the city, the frozen Moskva River glistening like glass under the stone bridge. As the paved roads transitioned into dirt roads, it took around an hour before they reached a wooden house in the Moscow suburbs. From this vantage point, one may be able to see the famed Kremlin, which towering spires and gleaming domes watched over the city. In comparison, there was nothing of note to be observed from the residence, which puzzled Ruiz as to the nature of their sudden trip outside the city. Was it perhaps someone Haze knew?

As it turned out, the valet's assumptions were not entirely correct. When the door opened, the gentleman did not recognize the young woman clad in a fur coat and a headscarf who welcomed them. It became clear that the lady was unable to understand English, but the conversation proved short somehow. With a thin smile, Haze bowed to the resident and once more turned to the Russian coachman, who was apparently told to wait. Ruiz was closely following him, although even he was still in the dark concerning his master's itinerary. Then again, it was not as if their relationship had changed in the past few days. As his faithful follower, he had to see the journey through, or at least until he could deliver the revolution funds he took from the Bank of England.

They were back in the city, but not to find a lodging. The coachman dropped them off the Novodevichy Convent, a fortress-like monastery which meadows had become skating rinks because of the winter climate. With its towers surrounded by walls, the valet entertained thoughts of his master meeting a female friend who may have lingered in the convent. Alas, his hopes of witnessing a real-life romance in the Russian Empire were dashed when he saw his master stop at one of the tombs. There was no flair involving the tomb's design. With a cross engraved on top, the blackish grave had a simple inscription which bore the person's name, birth date, and the day of death. Looking at the gentleman, however, kept Ruiz from speaking. While no significant emotion was visible from his face, and his eyes were conveniently concealed by the fogging of his lenses, the grieving atmosphere which emanated from his persona was quite felt from the valet's perspective. At that moment, he realized that the buried person was important for his master, albeit Ruiz still struggled about how this made any sense. Perhaps a thought struck Haze to visit someone in Moscow?

When he had mustered the courage to remind his master of the time, a steam car pulled nearby. One could not miss the engine's howl as it miraculously operated in the midst of Moscow's cold temperature. Ever ready, Ruiz looked on to see who was about to approach them. Nonetheless, he was also careful not to jump into conclusions, for if he acted too quickly and the person was only passing by, he might get in a similar trouble as his master's did in Warsaw.

With an overcoat to cover his military uniform, the man from the steam car walked alone, despite seemingly escorted anyway by other uniformed personnel. As the bearded man went closer, the insignia bore by his uniform became visible. Ruiz's eyes widened when he recognized the epaulettes. There was no mistake. The rank was that of a general. A former soldier such as he did not need to speak the Russian language to know the severity of the situation, more so as his master was still absorbed in staring at the grave. The nervous Ruiz reached for his bag, ready to draw his sabre when push comes to shove. His mind raced to reconsider the possibilities, the latest incident at Warsaw being top in his suspected reasons. Each step of the Russian general felt like a countdown to heaven, the fate of their world tour hanging in the balance.

The general halted in their vicinity, which heightened the valet's tension. However, when Haze did not appear to notice the Russian's presence, the latter reached out his hand to grab his shoulder. It was at this point that Ruiz brought out his sabre, the tip dangerously close to the general's throat. Then again, the advantage was lost. The valet blinked when he saw the Russian already aiming a pistol against him with his other hand, as if he was on automatic. Startled, the gentleman leapt from them and landed awkwardly on the snow-filled ground.

"Kto ty?!" the general bellowed, his gun still aimed at Ruiz.

"Par Dieu!" the valet exclaimed, unafraid of the pistol, "If you wish to take my master here, you'll have to face my blade."

Realizing for the first time what had transpired, Haze recovered and went in the middle of the heating standoff, "Please, John! Show your respect! The good man isn't part of the secret police!"

"How can I be certain, sir?" Ruiz angrily responded without taking his gaze away from the general.

The gentleman gently turned to the Russian, "Ustupat', Dmitry. Spasibo."

With a dry smile, the general immediately pulled back and placed the gun in his holster. The valet, however, took a few more seconds before returning the sabre to its sheath.

"Izvinite," Haze held the Russian by the shoulder, "He's new."

He then introduced the man to his valet, "This is the War Minister of the Russian Empire, Dmitry Alekseyevich Milyutin."

A veteran of the Caucasian War, the knowledgeable Dmitry Milyutin rose to the powerful position of Minister of War in 1861 as his ideas on military reform and his analysis of the Crimean War had convinced the tsar that the Russian armed forces could be significantly improved still. Ever since, the policies implemented under Milyutin's ministry had been regarded as the most sweeping since Peter the Great almost two centuries prior. His role, however, in the Circassian migration due to the Caucasian War left a negative mark on his reputation as a reformist. The Circassians were a group of at least twelve tribes occupying the northeast portion of the Black Sea.

Thousands were believed to have died because of the brutal tactics employed.

Milyutin grinned at the gentleman, "I must say, Gospodin Haze, your Russian hasn't dulled."

"And your English," Haze replied as he patted the minister's back, "Superb."

When Ruiz realized that Milyutin was acquainted with his master, he knelt on the snowy ground, "Please forgive me for my insolence. Do what you must, seigneur ministre."

The minister raised an eyebrow, "We're no longer in the era of serfdom. With your skill, I'm amazed you settled for an assistant's job. If you were Russian, I would've made you a captain!"

He then wrapped an arm around Haze, "But if you choose to work for this man, you're in a more difficult position than serving in Siberia."

Haze lightly pushed Milyutin back and went to raise his valet, "That's quite enough. Get up."

Ruiz nodded before standing up and keeping his distance from the two men, who then looked at the tomb. It turned out to be the grave of Milyutin's brother, Nikolay, who died the year before.

"I have a feeling you'd search for my bratishka," the minister's emotions well concealed by his bravado, "He always was a reformer, much like yourself. I'm conservative compared to you two."

"Flatterer. Nikolay was a bigger reformer than people would ever credit him to be. But that's not the only reason you're here, is it?" Haze queried.

"Of course, my duties won't allow me to visit on his death anniversary. The holidays are my only relief. Finding you here is, how do I put this? A blessing."

"What do you mean?"

Milyutin snickered, "You don't think we have no idea about what you did in Warsaw. You gave us a pretty bad day with the press there."

"Only a few years ago," Haze sighed, "it would take London two weeks to learn of a foreign leader's death. How have the times changed when it didn't take two days for a regular punch-up at a train station to reach the world? What's next? Reports on people dancing like animals? O tempora, o mores."

"Ha! You, a believer of progress, wondering how fast the world is today?"

"Amuse me," the British gentleman folded his arms, "I know you're here for something else."

The minister raised his hands, as if imitating surrender, "Sharp as always, Richard. We've heard of your wager, of course, and you can find me surprised that you chose to travel through Russia. Germany, too."

"Why shouldn't I? It's the logical choice."

"L-logical?" Milyutin kept himself from laughter, "The gentleman Fogg travelled through the British Empire. That's logical. He's British. Yours is not too reasonable."

Haze frowned, "Yes, indeed. Your great Trans-Siberian just denied me a trip to Vladivostok and cost me invaluable time to win my bet."

What followed was a brief silence, the cold breeze providing a respite from the quietness. Milyutin understood the limitations of Russian infrastructure. He himself had misgivings about the Trans-Siberian and the routes connected to it, considering how it was the only viable lifeline of Russian troops on the eastern front. Peasant uprisings in between had already proven his point that more transport options should be made available, especially for military purposes, or else the rest of the empire would be cut off and national interests would be placed at risk.

Haze, meanwhile, was trying to keep calm. When he thought doors have closed upon learning of his friend Nikolay's demise, he unexpectedly got to meet his brother Dmitry. While his relationship with Dmitry was not as intimate, taking into mind the British gentleman's views on the Circassian migration, among other actions taken by the Russian Ministry of War, he knew he needed the minister's support. He was convinced the relatively good head start he gained should not be put to waste because of bureaucratic pressures. Then again, despite his experience, Haze was not as acquainted to Russian politics as he would be with British. One false move and he would not only soil the relations he had with the minister, but also jeopardize his entire wager. He would be fortunate to even be given a chance to leave the empire alive. This distrust of imperial power was not limited to the British. He also extended them to Germans and Russians.

Haze's calculations were temporarily put to a halt when Milyutin spoke, "The Trans-Siberian usually takes 10 to 15 days from Moscow to Vladivostok. Our trains have to go all the way through intense conditions. Surely you understand where we're coming from."

The gentleman nodded as the minister continued, "If you wish to compensate us the trouble we had at Warsaw, I can offer you a fully-paid express trip to the eastern end of the empire in exchange for giving us good media coverage."

"How can I possibly do that?" Haze shrugged, doing what he could to contain his thrill of the development, "All I have is a valet with me. And since when did the press matter to you?"

Milyutin lightly punched Haze's arm, "Quit playing dull, Richard. The press follows you everywhere! I'll make it easy to understand, da? We'll make you our unique dignitary, pay for your Trans-Siberian trip. We'll even waive your accommodation anywhere the line covers–"

The gentleman waved his index finger, "No stops. How many days will the express train run?"

"How does eight days sound?"

"Seven," was the quick reply of the British, "and the train has to leave today. Only then will I consider your offer. You don't have to cover my fare. I have sufficient funds."

A ticket in the Trans-Siberian would cost around 1,000 pounds. The fare would naturally be higher if the passenger took a first-class cabin, in an express train even.

"Are you hearing yourself? That's too much," the minister argued, "We need the time for refueling and resting our men. How about paying half-price? Will you settle for eight days then?"

"I'm willing to pay double if you can bring me across Russia in seven."

Milyutin rubbed his beard as he contemplated Haze's counteroffer. The designation as Unique Dignitary was part of their plan to portray Russia as a progressive nation. If they could successfully facilitate the gentleman's trip, they would have an opportunity to boast Russian industry and provide a definite blow to the world powers, many of which had underestimated the empire's reform and prosperity, especially considering their defeat in the Crimean War, their struggles with internal dissent, and the assassination attempt against the tsar. Then again, Haze was requesting quite a dangerous endeavor. Besides the speed, which would cut the usual running time to half, the line was not in the best condition for travel, the harsh winter and rebel activity being among the major worries. They could not afford to flop on this challenge. Was it possible that Haze was already on to them, thus daring them to a near impossible task?

After fixing his cufflinks, the minister dragged him to the steam car, Ruiz closely following them. To the valet, it appeared they have reached an agreement. Without putting it in writing, however, what were the assurances that his master would be treated well? The best he could do at this time was to keep his guard up for the unexpected. Soon enough, they were at the station. As the express train was being prepared, Milyutin urged Haze to have his photograph taken for publicity purposes. While the gentleman refused, there was no stopping the Russian press, who were hastily assembled to document what may be a record-breaking journey. It did not take more than a few minutes for the photographs to be taken. However, when the minister saw Haze and Ruiz paying the fare, he went to the booth and declared their status as Unique Dignitary.

"No, Dmitry," the British gentleman insisted, "I'll pay as the people do. If 2,000 pounds can help this marvel of progress improved further, I'm willing to contribute my fair share."

Ruiz, who had been finding ways to earn additional funds as they went, was about to protest about what could have been a thriftier affair. Besides, the money had to last the entire journey, and at this rate, Haze might be spending more than what he could win in his wager. Then again, he realized there was no stopping his master when he had committed to his decision.

Milyutin sighed as he handed them sealed documents, "At least bring this as evidence of your designation as unique dignitary. It will prove our support throughout the empire. Godspeed."

The Trans-Siberian train hissed, then its engines roared. They were off. If all went according to Haze's agreement with Milyutin, they would reach Vladivostok by Day 11, saving them a total of three days. While he entertained doubts, not of the minister, but of Russian capacity to keep the pledge, his conscious choice of going through the Russian Empire still indicated an acceptable level of trust that he was taking the fastest possible route to the goal. As for Ruiz, who had yet to find a way to communicate their incredible progress to his allies, he would busy himself with attending to his master's needs, as well as getting acquainted with the Trans-Siberian. While the design appeared different from that of German trains, the operating capacity did not seem to be far behind relative to its European counterparts. After all, if they could indeed cross the Siberian taiga in a week, then it would be a miracle of technology.

It did not take long, however, for the world to learn of the apparent Russian bet for the British gentleman. Haze being their Unique Dignitary reversed overnight the popularity he had acquired in Britain due to the Warsaw incident, with small demonstrations taking the streets calling him a Russian spy and proposing to Her Majesty's government to bar his return at all costs. While there were a select few who still stood by his side despite the news, his low profile prevented him from being defended well based on his track record. His rivals were also quick on the uptake, utilizing their networks to finance smear campaigns which built mainly on already existent public perceptions of him thus far. If this eventually led to disgruntled groups working towards keeping Haze from triumphantly returning, then it would be for their benefit. While they doubted the veracity of reports trickling from Moscow that Haze was making good progress, it would nonetheless be better in their minds to take any step to win the global race. As it turned out, they did not need to orchestrate a lot of the dirty work if they intend to bring Haze to a halt.

It had been six days since the British gentleman left London when they reached Achinsk after crossing the Volga and the Ob Rivers. For the most part, there was nothing in the scenery which piqued Haze's interest, although Ruiz seemed to be more perceptive than his master as he noted the religiosity of Orthodox Russians worshipping by the rivers. They did not appear to mind much the cold weather as the fervor of their faith was apparently enough to kindle warmth for their bodies as well. At any rate, they would feel like a passing mirage to an observer from a train operating at enormous speed. When Ruiz asked one of the engineers, he said they were sustaining 80 kilometers an hour, which did not give his master satisfaction when the valet reported this trivial note. Haze, however, kept the discontent to himself, as he figured hustling them to maintain top speed might be detrimental to the train and its passengers.

It was not as if there were a lot of innocent passengers which the Russian government would mind in that express train, however, as Ruiz discovered in his exploration that only one of the train cars actually held civilian passengers such as they. This car was filled with gaiety as poetry, songs, and dances dominated the scene even as the train moved at top operating speed.

The next two cars were filled with Russian soldiers. He did not even have a chance to know them as the uniformed personnel changed in almost every station they stopped, the disembarking and the embarking cycles being quite monotonous since they left Moscow. While the soldiers also found ways to enjoy themselves, such as through gambling and drinking, there was nothing much to note about their overall behavior. Every batch seemed to be preoccupied with their respective burdens as guardians of Russian order. The last three cars held prisoners, or so the soldiers said, who were meant to work on the tsar's priority projects. However, one of the passengers refuted this claim.

Dressed in a fur coat over his evening jacket, as well as a fur cap which failed to conceal his pigtail, the Chinese trader who introduced himself as Lin Feng spoke in a mix of Chinese and English, "Aiya, listen Fuan Xiansheng, between you and me, a lot of prisoners can't even lift a hammer. In truth, they're political enemies with ideas unacceptable to the shahuang, left in Xiboliya to die."

As he attempted to comprehend the Chinese words being used, figuring in the course of their conversation that shahuang referred to the Russian tsar, Ruiz nodded, "I see, but do you think our journey would be impeded by the presence of these prisoners?"

Feng then leaned closer and replied with a softer voice, "The shahuang always sends prisoners to Xiboliya in a regular basis. But today different. Stay close to me if you want to live."

"Wait, what does that mean?" the valet reached out to the Chinese trader.

A sudden explosion was heard from the front of the train, causing the vehicle to screech to a halt. At first, it was presumed that the engines failed to keep their top speed. However, when the passengers opened their respective windows to see, the train was still intact. Then again, a huge amount of snow covered the tracks. Ruiz was among those who were quick to realize that it was a manmade avalanche. If it was meant to impede his master's ambition, then Haze would be in trouble. Upon jumping from his seat to rush to this master, Feng called out.

"If you leave now Fuan Xiansheng, we can't assure your safety!"

Ruiz was unable to reply at this point. His mind was occupied by checking his master's well-being. As he waded in the sea of passengers scrambling to leave the train, the valet was finally able to reach the gentleman, who he witnessed as firmly seated in his cabin. This puzzled Ruiz, who was quick to gather their things before presenting himself to Haze.

"Monsieur, we have to leave, too," the valet frantically said, "The perpetrators might be after you."

The gentleman closed his eyes, "John, I have this one question first."

"This isn't the time–"

"You called me sir in front of Dmitry instead of the French honorific monsieur. Pray tell, what's your purpose in trying to hide your identity in the presence of my friend?"

Ruiz almost dropped the bags in shock, his mouth open yet no words came out. Had his master realized the nature of his ruse already?

Meanwhile, Haze nodded as he continued, "No matter. I understand that France had a bitter history with the Russians, but please don't let it cloud your judgment next time. Remember that I'm not only your master, but your friend. Let me know about these things in order to serve me better."

Interrupting their conversation was the similarly exhausted yet relatively relaxed Feng, "Aiya, there you are, Fuan Xiansheng! Jiayou before–"

"No," the master shook his head, "I made a gentleman's agreement with Dmitry. We can't renege on that deal even if it meant risking our lives on this train."

The trader frowned as he pointed at Haze, "Who's this guzhi de shagua?"

Feng was then confronted by the gentleman in a modest manner, "Don't think I can't understand what you just called me. I've been to Hong Kong and Beijing."

Before they even got to be acquainted with each other, incomprehensible yells were heard from outside the train, immediately followed by clashing of weapons and firing of rifles. This convinced Ruiz that mortal danger awaited if they lingered in the Trans-Siberian any longer. Being virtually in the middle of a winter nowhere, the valet decided to drag his master along to follow Feng. Besides, what alternative was there other than the train? If this Chinese trader was confident of his chances in surviving the ordeal, it would be better to take the stranger's risk. However, what would the implications be for Haze's bid to tour the world in 80 days or less? Mundane affairs swirled away from their thoughts as survival became a more significant priority.

Strengthen Thyself

"Ni hao. In the name of His Imperial Majesty Tongzhi Huangdi, General of the Chu Army Zuo Zongtang, Qinchai Dachen of the New Frontier, welcomes you."

Dressed in a flowing changshan or long shirt, the Chinese general laced with court beads in the neck emerged from his encampment to cordially meet Feng's guests. As it turned out, Feng was serving as a double agent for the Chinese armed forces. Many of the soldiers in the Chinese camp, similarly dressed in changshan albeit not as grandiose nor intricate as that of Zuo, looked at them with astonishment. It appeared they never saw Europeans, modishly dressed in fact, who were far off in the Russian hinterland.

The mustachioed Zuo, however, was quite accustomed to the appearances of foreigners. After surveying them from head to toe, he waved his hand to summon a meal to be prepared in their midst. Almost immediately, a tent was set up, complete with tables, chairs, and even a sumptuous dinner. The main attraction, it seemed, was deep-fried chicken seasoned with soy sauce, garlic, scallion, and chili.

"Please, have a seat," the general invited them as he seated.

"Thank you for your hospitality," Haze calmly replied, "But we're in terrible hurry, Qinchai Dachen. We shan't keep you any longer if you allow us to return to the Trans-Siberian train."

Zuo frowned as he rubbed his chopsticks, "I believe that's not possible."

"The reason being?"

The general took a bite of his food before responding, "The train to Vladivostok is permanently cancelled from here on out. We demolished the tracks by making the train explode."

Ruiz looked with worry at his incensed master who thundered, "What have you done?!"

The Chinese soldiers leaped into action, pointing their rifles and swords at the foreigners.

"You won't survive an affront to Qinchai Dachen," Feng shrugged, "Jixu cautiously."

The general, meanwhile, commanded after taking more of the chicken that was served, "Shaoxi."

Acknowledging his order, the soldiers retreated back to their position by the Eight Banners, the military standard which flew as they were touched by the cool Russian breeze.

Zuo then continued, "I believe you're not in the position to negotiate, Sir Richard Haze."

The valet protested, recalling that he had not even introduced the gentleman to Feng earlier, "How do you know my master?"

"Shuo cao cao, cao cao dao. We have eyes and ears everywhere," the general chuckled, "Even in the remoteness of Xinjiang, the New Frontier."

With a resigned face, Haze held Ruiz's shoulder, indicating that they take their seats as Zuo offered. The valet was quick to recognize the master's bidding even without hearing him speak.

"Very well," the master then stared at the general, "What are your terms?"

"Is that how you look at your saviors?"

"Would you care to elaborate, general?"

"That train was filled with prisoners marked for death," Zuo answered as he pointed at the camp where they kept the freed captives, "When the tracks separate at Lake Baikal, they would fabricate an accident to have them executed quickly. They'll disappear like nothing happened."

Haze clasped his hands in front of his face, "But general, you do realize I'm a unique dignitary of the Russian Empire, certified by the Minister of War himself. Surely, they won't harm us, and neither should you."

"Aiya!" Feng interjected even as he just swallowed his food, "That's where you're mistaken! Had I known you're Richard Haze, I'd have spirited you out of Aqinske, not on the way at Kelasinuoyarsike where the attack happens."

"Sad to say, the wily Milyutin got you," Zuo looked at a pocket watch while speaking, "Russia is supporting Muslim rebels between our boundaries, but they act as if they had no hand at it. At the moment, they have rushed troops into our border to reinforce their claims, taking advantage of our weakness in Xinjiang to expand their territory south. Trains which should've run only daily have ramped it up, sending twice as many recently. Thus, instead of being accused of something we haven't done, we went ahead and took the fight here."

Haze was speechless, but Ruiz felt there was something off in the general's argument, "What's got to do with us, seigneur general? Why target our train in particular?"

The general pumped his fist, "To thicken the plot, of course."

"C'est pas possible!"

"But it is," Zuo gave a hearty laugh, "We're going to steal the thunder from the shahuang and give honor to our huangdi by transporting you to Beijing. From there, you can continue in your journey without any further intrusion from us. We take the glory, and you move onward."

"But—"

Ruiz was stopped by his master, who seemed to have recovered from his earlier surprise after tasting the chicken which surprisingly did not lose much heat despite the winter clime.

"No matter," Haze said, regaining his composure, "Dmitry promised to take us to Vladivostok in seven days. If you can't overcome that offer, I don't think there would be any agreement."

"Ah, yes," the general tapped his head and his chest, "I thought you had more faith in the colonized peoples than what your countrymen credit you?"

"The Chinese Empire, an imperial power, colonized?"

"Your nation of Britain defeated us in two wars," Zuo elaborated, his face reflecting the hardship Chinese leaders had to endure in balancing domestic and foreign affairs, "As we speak, other European nations do the same, short of calling it actual colonization. We made a lot of concessions to the great powers because they're interested in dividing up Zhongguo like Feizhou."

"Point taken," Haze replied, "I didn't mean to express my doubts on your situation. It's more like my lack of familiarity around these parts. I've been to Beijing, yes, but what else than the Trans-Siberian can transport us at peak speed?"

The valet also tried to recall on Haze's research if there were any other viable transport options in the area. The general, however, saved them the trouble of trying to figure that out. He asked one of his men to unfurl a map with markings in Chinese, Russian, and English.

Pointing at Krasnoyarsk, Zuo's finger traced what seemed like broken lines to Beijing, "It's estimated to be 4,000 kilometers from here to the capital, but we have a railway attached to the Trans-Siberian which crosses through Dongbei."

"Manchuria," Ruiz interrupted, "You mean Manchuria?"

"No, Dongbei," the general sternly answered before continuing, "The Europeans have conveniently deleted from any of their maps the railway they constructed by virtue of concession to hide how deep they have penetrated the empire. We have to make maps for our own use."

"I understand," Haze closed his eyes as he spoke, "Now it's quite clear to me how you can manage to actively campaign this far out in terms of geographical distance. But as for the speed…?"

Zuo smiled wide, his mustache almost seemed alive, "Everything is operating well. We can take you there by military train. You'll be in Beijing in three days at the latest."

The valet was amazed, but not his master, who remarked, "With all due respect, that's not too encouraging. Beijing is twice as far from Yokohama as Vladivostok is. I'm also aware of your recent tussle with the Japanese. How can you ensure safe passage for us if we're coming from China?"

The general's eyes widened, "Oh, you're observant of world affairs, I see. Unfortunately, yes, Meiji Japan has been quite belligerent lately, first with the issue of Chaoxian, and now Taiwan."

Haze nodded as Zuo continued, "But we'll uphold whatever pledge we make in the name of His Imperial Majesty. We'll secure you a neutral ship for your safe passage in Japanese waters. You'll be in Yokohama from here in at least a week. What do you think of this proposal?"

The gentleman narrowed his eyes, "That's generous of you considering I can't really negotiate. But would you mind if I ask this."

"Go ahead, Sir Haze," the confident Zuo smiled.

Looking away, the gentleman queried, "What will happen to the prisoners who were with us in the train? Will you take care of them?"

This startled the general, "Zhe shi shenme yisi?"

"You heard me, Qinchai Dachen," Haze gazed at the other camp which Zuo pointed earlier, "I don't mind if my life is put at risk, but if you intentionally placed them in harm's way to have an ace against the Russians, I can't ignore such a dishonorable action."

Ruiz tried to dissuade his master from speaking any further with incomprehensible whispers, but Zuo somehow realized what Haze was trying to say, "What Lin and I said are the truth. Our primary objective was to sabotage the railway, but not at the expense of the people who the shahuang had maltreated because of their progressive views. Progress doesn't wait for anyone in this new world order. If Russia won't accept them, I'll gladly take them under our fold. Zhongguo needs more of them as we look towards the future."

"But then, you're out here dealing with *rebels*? Isn't this their ancestral land to begin with? Certainly, they have a cause to fight, if it meant taking Russian assistance. What about diversity?"

"The Eight Banners are the symbol of our diversity. But without unity," the general replied as he turned his eyes to the map of China, "we can't move onward. I believe in the vision of the Ziqiang Yundong, and His Imperial Majesty has provided us more support than anyone else before him to successfully carry it out. If these rebels are in the way, we have to deal with them accordingly. They have unknowingly become tools of the shahuang's oppression by accepting Russian aid, resisting the reforms of the New Frontier for their antiquated ideas. You understand, don't you?"

Zuo then went on to describe how after the tsar emancipated the serfs, they were subjected to even more intense exploitation by their former lords, who now found them with less land and even lesser income. It was not long until some of the serfs opted to be reintegrated in larger estates, if only that meant they would be able to earn slightly higher wages than they would have received had they continued working their own land, but there were also others who chose to arm themselves and oppose the Russian government for failing to secure the future of the freed peasants. Had the process of emancipation begun earlier, internal conflict might not have escalated as quickly because more time was provided to better facilitate the transition from serfdom, including the provision of adequate support for the inevitable technological shift. The Ziqiang Yundong, or the Self-Strengthening Movement, was touted by its proponents in China as the solution for the empire to catch up to the world and provide a viable alternative to the regimes of other world powers, including Russia, Japan, and Britain. Opponents, however, did not share the optimism of the reformists. They looked down on the movement as a process of Westernization and allowing foreign incursion than actually building up their national strength.

Zuo himself, while coming from a scholar family who thrived in the past era, was not as fortunate to flourish in the old system as he achieved a rank no higher than a *juren* in the imperial examinations. A process known for its extreme difficulty, the exam's passing rates ranged to as low as 0.1 percent. The said rank, which literally translated to "recommended person," was not among the highest in the hierarchy, as it meant that Zuo was only a passer of the provincial level exams. In turn, he focused his efforts in practical skills such as farming, milling, and military training. Ever since, he had been fighting for the Qing while working on building economic activity in the areas he served. The Ziqiang Yundong allowed the likes of Zuo to be able to undertake foreign studies, his notable service in establishing the Fuzhou Arsenal further south in 1867 making him encounter on a regular basis a significant number of European experts, including the British and the French. This meant he also had to learn their languages, at least to an acceptable working level, so as to ensure they were not being taken advantage of in the long term.

While Haze took his time to consider the general's offer, gunfire was suddenly heard nearby, immediately followed by the galloping of horses. Russian troops, accompanied by Hui and Uyghur warriors, had broken through Chinese lines and were on vengeful fervor to wipe out what they viewed as inferior forces. Without a moment to lose, Zuo ordered Feng to take the two gentlemen to the nearest station and safely escort them to the Chinese capital. The trader was given an escort with horses at the ready. Despite the protests of Haze and Ruiz, the Chinese soldiers spirited them away, Feng following closely with a horse of his own. The last they would hear of Zuo's camp was the use of artillery fire, which then resulted to an uneasy silence as they rode on to their next destination.

It did not take long for them to see the Chinese train patiently waiting by the platform. The smoke coming from its chimney indicated it was quite ready to go at the soonest possible. While it was not as large nor as comfortable as any of the European trains they have tried thus far, Ruiz was more concerned about the speed with which it could continuously operate when the train finally departed. Haze, however, had momentarily set aside his thoughts on the wager for another matter. The British gentleman contemplated on the impetus of the reform movements in China and Russia, which to his comprehension appeared to be moving separate ways. Both nations were bent on catching up to the rest of the world powers, but beset by internal dissent and national issues, they appeared to have developed distinct views of reformation and innovation. For someone who saw British leadership of the world's progress as a necessary prerequisite, he wondered if development could ever be uniform among nations. Never mind Milyutin's ulterior motives. Haze believed that human rights and freedoms should weigh more than distant friendships, for as there were no permanent allies among nations, so there may well be no lasting friends among people.

Regardless of what the valet did to placate his master's peculiar behavior after the meeting with the Chinese general, it did not seem to make a dent through what seemed like an impenetrable barrier of thoughts. Leaving the gentleman be, Ruiz took his time trying to converse with the Chinese soldiers, which did not result to any productive outcome. It was either they respected him as the general's guest or because they understood from his words next to nothing. They resorted instead to filling their stomachs with hastily prepared soup and root crops.

Turning to Feng, who did his best to conceal his concerns about the recent attack, Ruiz asked, "Isn't there any other foreigner in this train with whom I can have a good chat?"

The Chinese trader snickered, "I'm here, ah. Not enough for you, Fuan Xiansheng?"

When the valet tried to avert his eyes, Feng followed up, "The engineer's British. But doubtful you'd want to distract him."

"I guess so," Ruiz gave up on the matter, "What is then next for us?"

"We'll see," Feng's reply left a chilling effect, for it felt like even the Chinese were uncertain at this point of where the gamble would lead.

Beijing turned out to be a massive city. While thick walls surrounded it, industrialization had also begun to creep into the ancient capital. Factories, mills, and telegraph stations sprouted in the midst of markets, religious shrines, and administrative centers. There was little to hear from foreign languages, or at least those which sounded European. In fact, even some of the European-looking blokes they saw spoke Chinese, albeit with seemingly atrocious accents at times because the locals did not understand. To be fair, the Chinese language was not a monolithic bloc. Speakers from Beijing might sound differently when compared with speakers from Hong Kong, but even a well-travelled person such as Ruiz may fail to correctly distinguish them the first time. Many walked on foot, talking as they went, although some chose to ride human-powered vehicles called rickshaws. They were believed to be imported technology, newly introduced by the Japanese who began to pour in the country in at least the past five years. For one who had seen mechanized vehicles in action, Ruiz could not fathom how the Chinese could choose to subject fellow humans to such laborious tasks. Then again, when he saw how the non-Chinese also use them, he was even more appalled.

When Feng saw how the sight of rickshaws peeved his foreign companion, he opted to find a way to escort them unnoticed. Thus, he persuaded them to change into changshan as well before leading them to Zijincheng, the Forbidden City, which housed the palaces of the Qing. Designed with a rectangular layout, Beijing could be witnessed in full view from any of its towering halls. A result of centuries of Chinese architecture, the structures were believed to be capable of holding itself against any known calamity to man, from typhoons to earthquakes. However, there were silent thinkers inside the city who believed that its durability was being translated quite differently to a dangerous extent. After all, the imperial administration was burdened not only by foreign incursion, but also by the weight of a growing nation.

It was an honor for commoners to even be able to set foot in the place, but neither Haze nor Ruiz realized it at the time. What the master understood, however, was that Feng's detour was taking quite a lot of time. While they saved around half a day as they dashed for their lives from the Russian front, it felt like it was not an enduring pledge of harmony that they were being detained against their will, and also against the purpose of the wager to be won.

Going into the Wuyingdian, one of the halls in the Forbidden City, a bearded man also dressed in changshan greeted them, "Da jia hao. Welcome to Zhongguo, venerable guests. We've been expecting you. I'm Grand Secretary Li Hongzhang, Zhili Zongdu, here to represent His Imperial Majesty, Tongzhi Huangdi."

Similar to Zuo, Li was one of the proponents of the Self-Strengthening Movement. This would also explain how he was adept with other languages, English included, as he had dealt with foreigners quite frequently. The room where they met the Grand Secretary reinforced the impression concerning his commitment to modernization as foreign maps, translated books, and miniature models of new technology were visible within the painted walls. Even the lightbulb which Ruiz first saw in Haze's house was also present in the room, albeit Li only had one of them in display along with the numerous lanterns which lit the spacious place. Similarly painted dividers were in the room, but they were apparently moved to the carpeted sides.

While Ruiz bowed low in reverence, the observant Haze did not seem to understand protocol. This raised Li's eyebrow, who was quite confident of his intelligence that the British gentleman had been to China before. Feng took the cue from the Grand Secretary, nudging the valet to notice his master's unruly behavior in front of the Qing's top officials.

"Monsieur," Ruiz whispered to the gentleman, "Please regard the Grand Secretary."

Haze shot a quick glance at the valet, who backed off almost immediately, before speaking to Li, "General, or rather, Secretary Li, I'm certain you're aware of my great haste. I don't have time for formalities."

"I understand," he smiled, disregarding the gentleman's lack of respect, "But please, before you go, would you like to meet the benefactor of all the reforms we've had in recent years, Tongzhi Huangdi? I can arrange for–"

"No matter," the master waved a hand and turned away, "If your emperor wishes to know of my views of Ziqiang Yundong, I'm not the best person to consult. I am but a humble advocate of reform. Nothing more. I believe if there's anyone who would know better the conditions of the nation, it would be your people. Now, if you would be so kind to excuse us, Secretary."

"Sir Haze," Li walked in front of him and gave him a box, "A keepsake, in exchange for a photograph of you in the city. I implore you. The ship is ready to sail from Tianjin after this."

Haze narrowed his eyes, "You may do so."

After taking the quick photograph, officiated by a Frenchman, the master approached the Grand Secretary, "Now is not the time to look at Europe or America for inspiration. We may well be as conservative as many among your people, and this will make it a difficult affair for all of us. This is why I'm afraid I have nothing new to offer to your cause. But the likes of you and General Zuo leads me to believe there is hope for progress not only in China, but for the world."

This sudden statement baffled Li, who was only able to say, "Xiexie, Sir Haze. That's kind of you."

"We may not know the future, but as long as we seek the betterment of all, we are in a good direction. Take strength from this, Secretary Li. Not one soul should be left behind."

With those parting words, Haze and Ruiz left the Chinese mainland altogether. Despite Chinese generosity, the gentleman still insisted to pay for the fare. The partly armored commercial ship they embarked on, however, heightened the valet's insecurities. It turned out to be a Spanish ship called El Sexto Niño. Seeing the Spanish flag flying in the mast eventually caused Ruiz to collapse, much to his master's surprise. He did not witness Ruiz ever having seasickness in Wenn Im August, making him wonder what could have been the matter. Was it perhaps the change of climate? While they have already sailed, it was fortunate that a doctor was on board, or at least she claimed to be one. The Filipina medic who served as de facto resident doctor of the ship since it left the Philippines did not exactly receive her license to practice.

However, she believed her experience was quite sufficient to compensate for her lack of corresponding certifications. With no other feasible choice, the reluctant Haze entrusted his valet to her as he proceeded to his cabin, occupying himself with planning how to conduct their journey after Yokohama. They expect to reach the Land of the Rising Sun by Day 13, a few days earlier than initially projected, perhaps in no small part due to the troubles they met along the way. His meeting with Li, and the keepsake given by the Grand Secretary, contributed to lifting the fog of uncertainty that had once blocked his resolve.

Upon opening the intricately designed box, Haze found a fan which bore inscriptions in Chinese. On one side, the concessions and the unfair treaties enforced by the foreign powers. On the other side, the successful reforms of the Self-Strengthening Movement. While his knowledge of Hanzi was quite limited, causing him to fail reading some of the written characters, he nonetheless managed to understand the gist of the text. As he leaned back and used the fan to ease the heat in the cabin, memories of his earlier trip to China filled his mind. After surviving the debacle at sea aboard Rossa's Sekunden in Moll, Haze found himself in Hong Kong, where he became one of the first investors financing a local bank to accommodate British merchants. His adventurism in business, however, led him to be leered by his countrymen.

The keen Haze felt the environment had shifted against him, but when he was about to leave Hong Kong, his enemies among British circles managed to fabricate charges which could have caused his incarceration. A local Chinese official, meanwhile, saw through the merchants' plans. Asserting that Haze committed another crime outside British-held territory, another fake claim as well, the Chinese managed to remove with a legal stroke the gentleman from the corner of his adversaries. Despite the argument of the merchants that a foreigner should be judged in their own territory even if he had done the act in Chinese land, citing supposed provisions which disallowed Chinese jurisdiction over non-Chinese violators, they eventually dropped the case and secretly delighted themselves with the prospect that Haze's blood would not be in their hands. The Chinese court presided by the said official proved lenient, much to their dismay. He would later learn that the official was one of the proponents of the Self-Strengthening Movement, which had just begun in the country and was just as fiercely opposed as it would be later on. Haze realized that reform once again saw faith in reason and saved him from the malicious hands of his opponents.

Then again, it seemed wherever he went, even if he chose to tour the world, conflict and envy always caught up with him. News of his presence in Beijing arrived in London at about the same time as that of the explosion in the Trans-Siberian line, which puzzled most spectators. The British government stalled to act despite the potential of a British citizen succumbing in an international accident as they probably knew only as much as any of the people who placed their bets on the race. His own rivals, Rausch and Plain, were likewise perplexed by the sporadic reports. Was it perhaps a double? Or possibly Haze had been killed in Russia? The extraordinary speed which suggested the British gentleman reached China in less than two weeks felt more whimsical than real. That would have meant travelling around 10,000 kilometers in all. A statistical impossibility. Even Phileas Fogg would have found it absurd.

At this juncture, Plain had been traversing the vast expanse of the United States, relishing the heroine's welcome as she remained confident of the efficiency of

American rail. Meanwhile, Rausch had already crossed the Ottoman Empire, the end of the European rail system in the east, and was already en route to India via ship. The two ladies believed the race was just between them from then on, but Haze was not to rest on his laurels too soon. The uniformed captain sporting a clean shave, a Spanish creole named Pascual Salamanca, approached the British gentleman in his cabin to inform him of falling barometric pressure. A sign that inclement weather was coming.

"The crew are already on alert, Señor Haze," Salamanca said, "But I can't risk running through a tempest for your haste. I've already made the decision and I'm asking you to adjust your schedule accordingly. We're taking a long detour south to avoid the East China Sea altogether, at least until the weather clears."

The gentleman studied his notes as he responded, "How long do you think would it last?"

"I can't say for sure, señor. We'll only have a better appreciation when we get ashore."

A January storm would be a rare occurrence in the Western side of the Pacific Ocean. The northeast monsoon would have gained strength in the area by this time of the year, making it difficult for any typhoon to gain significant devastating power even if it did form. However, it was not to say the phenomenon was impossible. Apparently, high pressure areas in Japan and the Philippines gave the weather disturbance no choice but to plow between and cross the East China Sea before proceeding northwestward.

It was not yet a typhoon by meteorological standards, but it had nonetheless packed enough winds and rains for a ship its size to rethink its course. From rerouted trips to encountering the secret police to exploding tracks, the gentleman was now faced by the forces of nature to stop him in his tour of the world. With his trusted valet still out, who he would have expected to help him navigate in Asian lands, and confronted by virtual information blackout at sea, Haze would have to strategize on his own how to move in unfamiliar territory.

Auspicious Return

"Kumusta na ang iyong pakiramdam, Juan? Nakadalawang araw ka na."

As Ruiz slowly opened his eyes, he saw a seated woman donning a white apron over her dress, with her hair tied behind her by a handkerchief. Her dark eyes looked at him intently when he realized she called him by his original name and she spoke in good Filipino. Was he hallucinating? The last time he remembered, they were on a ship departing from Tianjin. How could he meet someone he knew in a supposedly neutral ship, especially as he had no chance to communicate his location to any of his allies due to Haze's hurry? The room certainly looked like a ship's cabin, so he sought an immediate explanation to clear up the misunderstanding.

"Pardon me," the valet weakly responded, "But who are you, mademoiselle?"

She sneered, "Pwede mo nang lisanin ang zarzuela na 'yan. Nalalaman ko na ang tunay mong pakay sa pagsisilbi mo sa kanya."

"Huh? What do you mean?"

She sighed before taking out one of his bags, "Señor Haze left here your bags. He must have realized how much you valued them, or rather, the content of these bags."

Ruiz tried to get up, but when his head hurt, he was unable to leave his bed, "You don't mean you pried in my belongings! You wretched witch!"

The lady lightly tapped his shoulder, "Is that how you thank your doctor?"

The valet frowned, "Doctor, you? Why, what happened to me?"

"A case of anaphylactic shock," she calmly replied as she laid down the bag, "The trigger, it seems, was the sight of La Rojigualda."

"That's ridiculous…"

"But," she shifted to a cheery mood, "I told them you're just tired from lack of good sleep."

"Should I really thank you for that?" Ruiz massaged his head, checking for signs.

She reached out her hand, indicating a desire to shake his hand, "Soy Aya Dimalaya, pero mi nombre ahora es Maria Mala Razon. Y tu?"

"Usted ya sabe," he said, rejecting her offer of a handshake.

She then took a slim notebook, "Juan Ruiz, Corporal, Fort San Felipe. For a former soldier, you're quite sloppy in keeping your things in order. I would've not known if you don't carry these revealing papers around. But why, I wonder, would a Castila such as you be in China, serving an Ingles as his señor?"

Out of instinct, he grabbed the notebook, only to find it was full of drawings and sketches instead of actual notes. He even saw one sketch of him sleeping.

"You cheat!" he yelled, "How much do you know?"

"Hoy, ikaw, nakakailan ka na talaga," she shot back, "I already put back the paper in your bag. I promise you I didn't touch anything else. Besides, the other bag looks quite heavy for someone who travelled often. I won't be bothered fixing it if something bad happens. La Caja de Pandora!"

Sighing with relief, he then collected himself to regard the doctor and return her notebook, "Doctora Razon, forgive me for my disrespect. I owe you this much, señora. I'm quite certain you have ideas why my body reacted in such a way when I laid my eyes on La Rojigualda."

"Ah, hindi señora," she waved her index finger, "Señorita pa ako. Mind your manners."

She then leaned towards him, "So, tell me, impatient patient. Are you a peninsular or an insular? Or perhaps an indio? You don't look—"

Ruiz shook his head, "I'm a Filipino."

Dimalaya gasped, "An exiled nationalist? Did you by any chance know about the Cavite Mutiny?"

"I'm quite aware, yes."

"No way... No wonder you fainted," she whistled, "Well, don't worry about me. I already set my sights abroad, but if you're planning to return to Filipinas now, you're in buena suerte."

"Why?"

She responded as she continued scribbling on her notebook, "The iron-fisted Izquierdo is out just last week, when we left Filipinas. Sick, they said, but I doubt it. Even illness would fear that man. MacCrohon is currently in charge, but I heard the king sent a new captain general. If he's arriving by ship, like this one we're on, he'll probably arrive sooner than later. I bet it'd be another soldier though. When will they send real governors there?"

Her words took time to register to him, but when they did, Ruiz's head turned as if it would be blown away. With eyes wide, he screamed while shaking her by the shoulders.

"Hijos del pais! Do you know what this means?!" the excited valet yelled, "A perfect opportunity! The revolution lives!"

The doctor slowly removed his hands from her, narrowing her eyes as if looking at a creep, "Si, si, I understand. A bit. I don't know what you love about that godforsaken colony... or do we call it province? Or whatever! But, I'm just glad I can pursue my goals elsewhere."

Realizing her apathy of the Philippines, Ruiz carefully asked, "You're a talented lady, pride of our nation. Yet you seem to have bad blood about your country. Our homeland. I won't persuade you to return, but if I may know, I'll eagerly listen to your story."

Dimalaya grinned at how the soldier flattered her while she handed over a glass of colored water, "Aha, you sure about that? Then drink this first."

The valet looked at the glass from top to bottom, then back to the top again, before snatching the glass from her and taking the drink with one go. This startled the doctor, who almost fell from her seat upon witnessing him daring her casual challenge.

"Aba, that wasn't so bad now, was it?" he remarked, "What's in it anyhow?"

"Ah... A special brew... For headaches... But why? What if? N-nobody trusted my recipes..."

Ruiz smiled, "A doctor is a doctor, regardless of who it is, regardless of where they are. No true doctor will put the patient in jeopardy. Now that you mention it, I feel better already."

She looked down, covering her eyes with one hand, "I wanted to leave because I'd never become a real doctor there. It isn't just the people who shame the wise and the earnest, the leaders make it difficult for social mobility. They deprived me of my license because of my views, because I'm a lady. Not even in España would they allow a woman, a colonial, to practice. This won't do, I thought. Britain licensed their first female doctor a decade earlier. Could you imagine?"

The valet nodded, "I understand. Soldiers like myself were also discriminated in the armed forces. Filipino soldiers have been professionalized since 1796, but we never felt so neglected. We've been relegated at least two ranks below our Castila counterparts from the peninsula."

With clenched fists and gnashing teeth, Ruiz continued his tirade, "Our confirmation papers could be delayed for years on end. So did our salaries. The military overflowed with pesos, and we didn't even get a centimo. They say we've ciudadania Española with constitutional rights and representation, but we're not being treated as citizens at all."

"You understand, right?" Dimalaya's eyes shone as she raised her head, "Oh, talaga, when I talk about this with literally everyone else, they just scoff at me. Like it's supposed to be the natural order of things. But Juan, you're different. Indeed, you are."

"Please," he sighed, "Don't call me by that name. My master knows me as John Ruy."

She winked, "Alright, *John*, what do you plan to do now?"

"I'd very much seek to return to Filipinas to take advantage of the regime change," Ruiz scratched his head, "But my master isn't just going places. He's in a race. I can't leave him hanging since he needed me. And right now, this ship is bound for Japan. That's close, yet so far."

The doctor looked away, "You didn't hear, did you?"

"Por favor?"

"Due to bad weather, El Sexto Niño was rerouted."

"Where? Where?!" he leaned closer to her even as she did all she could to avoid his gaze.

"T-teka! Taiwan. I think the captain said Taiwan."

Mustering all his energy, Ruiz somehow managed to rise from bed like a powerful spring, "Forgive me, Doctora Razon. Can you please do this favor for me? Please, I shan't have a moment to lose."

In a rush for shelter, the Spanish ship managed to reach Taiwan, a small island symbolizing the limit of Qing territory in the Pacific, after four days of sailing. While administered by the Chinese for centuries, the Japanese had been roaming the surrounding waters in the name of protecting its own people. Recently, fishermen sailing to Taiwan from Ryukyu were reported to have been imprisoned by the Chinese, even though they viewed the latter islands as part also of the empire. Japan, however, claimed sovereignty over Ryukyu as well, which they asserted was subsidiary to one of their domains, the Satsuma. The legal implications, however, have been complicated by the abolition of the domains. Should the new Japanese state also inherit the tributaries of the former domains? For a ship flying the Spanish standard, however, this situation seemed too distant to meddle with. It might be slightly larger than Wenn Im August, but it posed no significant threat for the competing interests in the area. Besides, the Spanish had long relinquished their claims over Taiwan. They were quite content with the economic benefits of navigation freedoms. Haze, however, was agitated when he learned of what had transpired as they entered Keelung harbor, situated in the northern part of Taiwan.

"What are you saying, Doctor Razon?" the gentleman was unable to calm down as he walked to and fro on the ship's deck, "First the storm, and now this? Why wasn't

I informed prior to this decision? Is that how you run things around here?"

Dimalaya bowed repeatedly, "It's an emergency, Señor Haze. We're merely human. And we're limited with what could be done in this island."

"No matter," Haze sighed, "When will his return be?"

The doctor stopped with her head still looking down on the wooden floor, "Ah, the thing is…"

And thus, the undercover valet had left his master and whatever funds entrusted to him by the British gentleman for good, with Haze helpless to influence what was already set into motion. Taking advantage of the night to get ahead of the ship and sneak into Keelung to prepare for his eventual return to the Philippines. Before leaving Keelung altogether, however, he utilized Filipino connections in the island to secure a way to communicate his plans to the revolutionaries who remained in the Philippines, as well as to Captain Azuchi, who had not heard from him since December. With the lines going through Hong Kong, Ruiz and his associates made it sure to cover their tracks. Even with Izquierdo's departure, the Spanish colonial government and its intelligence capacity must not be taken lightly, especially as they had organized five years prior the *guardia civil*, which was composed of military personnel essentially performing tasks similar to a police force. Their inputs would be part of the reason why Izquierdo suspected the Black Hand's presence in the Philippines. Also, being a majority Filipino force, it helped perpetuate what Spain had been conveniently taking advantage of for centuries to maintain hegemony over the Philippines: pitting Filipinos against each other.

He had already smuggled himself in a merchant ship to Manila, this time disguised as a British businessman with the name Joseph Smith, when the messages were received by the people he needed to communicate with. Azuchi, meanwhile, was in a training mission at Nagasaki when she was given the telegram. Nagasaki was located 1,200 kilometers south of Yokohama. As was her usual routine when reading personal messages, she shut herself in her room before opening the telegram with a mix of excitement and nervousness.

To the most excellent captain of Ryukansen,

My sincerest apologies go to you, as I am unable to write since our last. I know not if I could have the leisure after this, for I am now on my way to a famed restaurant. I was told a new chef was in town, so I saw it fit to pay a visit and spend a good amount to our satisfaction. It would be an opportune time to try new delicacies. Thereafter, I hope to see you again and share with you the happiness deserved by a good friend. No rainbow reveals its bloom without the generous pouring of rain.

Tempora mutantur, nos et mutamur in illis.

Warm regards, Risu Tsuringu.

After perusal, she crumpled the telegram and repeatedly pounded her fist on a table, "Baka! Are you literally sending me your last will?"

With the telegram still tormented inside her hand, Azuchi burst out of her room and went to the nearest telegraph station. Without regard for any of the operators in the office, she ordered to have a communication sent to the Ministry of the Navy in Tokyo.

"A message for the Kaigun Daijin," the fuming Azuchi bellowed, "Requesting immediate dispatch of the Ryukansen to Taiwan! Urgent matter of utmost action needed!"

"Chotto matte kudasai, daisa," the operator tried to halt the leaving captain, "Machimasen, eto, I mean, won't you wait for their reply?"

"I don't care what that two-faced Tokugawa dog says," she angrily responded, "I'm going."

Willing to break navy protocol for the sake of a foreigner, the captain then proceeded to her ship, wherein she gave the marching orders to the crew. In minutes, the ever-ready Ryukansen was off from Nagasaki waters, but even at top speed, it would prove too late to influence whatever Ruiz had in mind. Three days since leaving Taiwan, the merchant ship which concealed the returning soldier had arrived in Manila. With incredible stealth, he was able to slip past not only the customs guards, but also the strict quarantine enforcers, who suspected virtually everyone entering the city. Since the turn of the century, the Philippines had been ravaged by epidemics despite the introduction of vaccination for certain diseases. While the colonial government was quite aware of the mitigation techniques used elsewhere, improvements for public works and health systems were not included in the top of their agenda.

Among the latest to bring suffering was a cholera outbreak, which supposedly came from contaminated water, but was believed by some in the local population to have been brought by foreigners who did not adhere to the Roman Catholic faith. Thus, instead of avoiding crowds and sterilizing water, churches were filled from the inside out, and people fervently endeavored to be blessed by, among other things, water. Christian rituals, however, had also been subjected to syncretism as images of saints were also accompanied with amulets, talismans, anitos, glyphs, and even indigenized chants which may sound like Latin, but were actually in the vernacular.

Had the soldier arrived earlier, he would have to endure the sea of the faithful bearing the Black Nazarene for its annual *traslacion*, one of the foremost images of Christ in the Philippines, its name derived from supposedly being burned during its transfer via ship from Mexico. Of course, that origin story did not prevent people from forming their own theories on the miraculous image. He felt quite fortunate to have not encountered this, albeit the usual roster of religious processions for an archipelago which essentially had a feast for each day of the year were quite sufficient for him to remain on guard. Besides, Ruiz did not seek to involve civilian population in what he thought would be a military operation. Their religious fervor, long buttressing Spanish rule in the Philippines, might even turn people power against the revolutionary cause.

Suburbs surrounding the walled city, meanwhile, were signs of increasing urbanization. While wooden houses still sprawled in the landscape, towering structures of stone and concrete which reminisced that of European cities had also begun to make their marks, some functioning for production purposes, while others catering the growing service and retail industries. Much like the crammed capital, however, the more spacious suburbs also showed signs of congestion as the Spanish imprint began to mix quite well with other cultures. One might even suspect that the Spanish cared little about "Hispanizing" daily affairs outside their seemingly medieval center mainly composed of stone forts and steel churches. They were Spanish settlements only in name.

Soon enough, after exiting Intramuros, a man clad in barong and trousers had been waiting to meet up with Ruiz in a local panciteria, which did not only offer noodles as the place name suggested, but also had a variety of offerings for locals and foreigners alike.

Seated on a little wooden stool, the man was quick to offer him pie, "Tarta de coco, hmm?"

"No tengo hambre, pero gracias," the soldier replied as he took his seat, "Como estas, Samuel?"

Samuel took a bite before responding, "Estas seguro… podemos hablar en Español?"

"Porque? Los Chinos no entienden."

Without looking, the man motioned his head towards some of the boisterous students talking in Spanish and eating with them in the place, "Pero ellos? Ellos podrian cantar canciones."

"Fine then," Ruiz slightly raised his hands, "English?"

Samuel pointed at his nose, "Proceed. You know well I can't understand your Franses."

"Can we do it on the 20th?"

The man frowned as he stared at his tea, "You mean, the anniversary? Isn't it too early? We won't have time to prepare."

Lightly tapping the wooden table which had a Chinese character engraved on it, Ruiz argued, "But if the new general arrives before we take action, wouldn't it be all for naught? He'll surely bring in new officers, less relaxed than the ones we have now. Think of it, Samuel, the money is with me. We can pay anyone who can assist us for this. We can bring in an ironclad with the right price. We're more prepared than you think."

The confused Samuel scratched his head, "I heard they're sending Alaminos. He's got a liberal record like de la Torre. Maybe we could try bargaining–"

"No, Samuel," the soldier placed a palm on his face, "We've already discussed this. No matter what *Madre* España does, Filipinas will always be behind. We're like a child left for dead, expected to survive on our own wits than cherished until able. We might as well chart our destiny."

"Alright, I understand," the man tried to calm Ruiz, "Still, we haven't got the best men in our corner yet. We're trying to convince the regiments to rise up, but only those in the provinces gave encouraging replies. The most crucial ones, those guarding Intramuros and the arrabales, are not for us at this time. Even Mirong's tulisanes won't lend us their aid, and they gave the government a hard time the past decade. As for the foreigners, only the Germans were quite amenable, but they seemed to be concerned with Mindanao first.

American, Chinese, British, and French business thrived here. I don't think they want España out."

Casimiro Camerino, infamously known as the legendary *El Tulisan* or "The Bandit" to Spanish authorities, had terrorized surrounding areas of Manila with his elusive tactics and his charismatic leadership. He himself was regarded as a force in the battlefield, being reportedly adept with either melee or ranged weapons. The end of his struggle, however, would not come by means of force, but by mantle of reform. Izquierdo's predecessor as captain general, the reformist Carlos Maria de la Torre, was instrumental to the creation of the guardia civil in 1868 with Camerino as one of its top officers. To this day, despite Izquierdo's brutal policies, the formerly rebellious leader remained in the service of the guardia civil, albeit the more suspicious in the upper echelons of the colonial administration still doubted the erstwhile rebel's loyalty.

"Even in suffering, the needs of the flesh would always overwhelm the desires of the heart. They'll join sooner or later, especially when we win," Ruiz responded as he placed his hands in front of him, "What we need is a kind of shock tactic to bring them down like lightning. This will circumvent our inferiority in numbers. Novales almost succeeded with this. We can do better."

"Don't think of the tulisanes that way. They may not be soldiers like us, but still, they're veteran warriors. Besides, we can't bring a ship to Manila Bay, even if it's made of steel," Samuel muttered, "It'll be a sitting target for the guns of Intramuros."

The soldier nodded as he handed over an envelope, "Let's meet in Cavite two days from now. Tell them this would be their first payment. Expect more if they could do better recruitment."

"Two days? Tomorrow, you mean?"

"You know what I mean, Samuel."

"You're not cheating us now, are you?" the concerned face of Samuel caught Ruiz's eye.

"The only lie we ever believed was the loving care of the government."

Upon parting ways, Samuel went to an alley, making sure he was not followed nor seen, before checking the package. It was even more spectacular than he hoped. It was literally flowing with pound sterling, an amount which could have allowed him to retire for the rest of his life. He was no longer an engineer for the military, after all, but he still scraped daily in order to sustain a living. Just then, the thought dawned on him. The revolution was never a sure thing, but the money with him was already a certain jackpot. Even winning the lottery could not compare with this. Would it not be easier for him to betray his friends and live peacefully? Then again, the traitor Saldua died nonetheless despite earning well as an agent under the pay of the Spanish. What if the same fate awaited him for running away with the funds of the revolution?

As for Ruiz, he was quick to change his disguise once more to reassume the character of Joseph Smith. He would then find himself at the residence of the British consul, who received him quite congenially upon being informed of his background as a businessman. Fortunately for him, the consul was relatively new, and had somehow believed that he just returned to the Philippines. This, however, took a persuasion stage wherein Ruiz had to flaunt a bit of his wealth. In the Philippine economy, the Spanish were not the most competitive, but the British, who were even lobbying for a railway to be built under the influence. Only a few years earlier, the first telegraph line was laid to foster better communications. While it was exclusively for military use initially, the Philippines would later find commercial benefits from this, and the British sought to profit as the archipelago embarked through the path of technological progress.

Leaning on the rail of his balcony, which overlooked Pasig River and the telegraph station shining brightly because of the newly installed gas lamps, the consul beamed, "What is the nature of your business again, Mr. Smith?"

"Corrugated galvanized iron, which the Spanish may call as *hierro*," Ruiz replied as he also placed a hand on the balcony's railing, "And shoes as well."

Glancing at the false businessman's shoes, the consul commented on its apparent quality, "It doesn't look like a Chinese production to me. Are you sure the labor is sourced locally?"

Ruiz nodded, "And hierro would soon take over nipa houses, you see. They're more durable, and can be mass produced. We're developing future industries here, so I won't be surprised if you haven't heard from us yet, Excellency."

"If it's recognition from the consulate you need," the consul puffed a cigar, "You don't have to talk with me about that. Spain should be the one worrying about the registration hullabaloo."

"To be frank, Your Excellency," the false businessman shifted to a serious tone, "I've received credible information about the prospects of Spanish rule in Filipinas. I heard that the interim captain general is planning to prevent the arrival of a liberal replacement by faking a revolt."

"What's that got to do with us? You're making less sense, my good chap."

"This," Ruiz handed over a forged pamphlet which appeared like an order of battle plotted on a map, "The Spanish here always envied our industriousness. As they once flushed the Chinese out, they also plot to take down all the consulates during the upheaval. Once they have spooked us and the others, they'll sequester the factories and the businesses we painstakingly built. Your Excellency, we can't possibly allow the crafty Spanish to do their bidding in Asia. They thought that by opening up Manila, they'd be able to garner a good share of the pie in Pacific trade, but since they realized their economic plans backfired, they're aiming against us."

After taking another cigar, the consul argued, "That's quite a bold claim, Mr. Smith. Even with this evidence at hand, I can't bring myself to easily believe this horrible conspiracy."

"If you don't wish to take my word for it, you may consult with the other consuls about this. Something this massive might have already reached their ears as well. Thank you for your time, Excellency," Ruiz shook the consul's hand before taking his leave.

Unbeknownst to the British consul, Ruiz had already taken his time to also play his ruse with the other consuls and foreign representatives in the city. Each time, he assumed another identity and donned a different outfit, wisely using his knowledge of other languages to suit the needs of the ploy. As he expected, the foreign dignitaries were in agreement. They all received similar details concerning the Spanish conspiracy, and the paranoia it brought was realized. Fortunately, they thought, the date of the supposed revolt staging was given to them. They did not have to speculate any further. Acting for the first time in unity, the consuls who were once suspicious of each other gave urgent distress calls to their respective governments, requesting assistance to be brought to the Philippines at the soonest possible. While it would take time for the decision to be reached, once a world power sent something to the Philippines, others would likely follow suit. The scramble for the door to Asia was on.

It had been nineteen days since Haze left London for a race around the world. Ruiz, however, was already convinced that even without his presence, the gentleman would be able to finish the task and accomplish it wonderfully. After all, he barely did anything to help Haze overcome the challenges thrown at his plate. He wondered at times why the gentleman even needed a valet. There was no time, however, for regrets. The signal for the second wind of the revolution was about to be made. When their agents had successfully cut the cable connecting the Philippines to the world, the lights of

Manila would be shut at the same time fireworks would illuminate the skies. The very tactic which duped them in the mutiny last year would this time be used against their enemies. Instead of a jovial feast, a hail of bullets welcomed the affair.

"Viva Filipinas! Viva la Independencia! Viva la Revolucion!" Ruiz and the soldiers who had discarded their loyalty for Spain yelled as they charged.

Their march from Malate, which was south of the city, was not the only force which confronted the loyalists. From the north, another regiment marched from Tondo, and from the east, a group of hired mercenaries from Camerino's former bandit group rushed from San Juan. While seemingly less equipped than their professional counterparts, they proved to be well trained. Some of them were known as *arnisadors* or *eskrimadors*, making them adept with any weapon which may come to mind. Such was the skill of those who immersed themselves in Filipino martial arts that they were believed to fight fiercely and efficiently even with bare hands. One may wonder how they managed to hold out for the longest time against the Spanish despite being an inferior armed force on paper, and this would probably be a reason why.

To make matters worse, a commercial ship which traversed the Pasig River was reportedly emerging from Laguna de Bay with hastily equipped artillery pieces. Other contingents in the provinces across the archipelago, many of which were composed of Filipino integrees, also began to rise up and overwhelm the numerically inferior Spanish officers. It would be difficult to coordinate with them considering the prevailing constraints, but the strategic objective was to keep the Spanish guessing where to focus their limited strength. The returning corporal was beginning to see the fruits of a well-financed revolution, but nagging his mind as they fought the token resistance thus far was how much impetus would the profit motive provide to fuel their movement. Unlike the reformists he met in Haze and his acquaintances during their brief journey together, it did not appear to him that many who rose with them were driven by any other cause than filling up their rumbling stomachs. Had they fully realized what it really meant to be Filipino? To chart the arduous path towards a free and independent nation?

The Spanish would not be taken by surprise for long, however, as they train their guns against the insurgents. Firing, however, was halted by the sound of ships anchoring not from the Pasig River, but from Manila Bay. Terror took over as the soldiers were uncertain where to target. Were they contracted to demolish Intramuros? The ships, conveniently shrouded by the darkness of the night, turned out to be the assistance requested by the respective consuls. Except the Germans, which brought a cruiser, a corvette, and a supply ship, bringing the total to three, the rest of the foreign powers sent one cruiser each. Ruiz could only be delighted inside his heart. The Spanish once cheated them into believing that America sent one of its ships to Manila, a likely scenario which once opened up Japan. They were now being given their own medicine.

As they entered Intramuros, it was a breath of fresh air for the former soldier, and he felt the spirit of his superior, Sergeant Lamadrid, was guiding the light of liberty for them. It was at this juncture, however, when the organization of his hastily assembled army began to crumble. Witnessing how the panicked Spanish, who had no memory of a successful revolt ever taking the colonial capital, ran like roaches without heads, Ruiz lost effective control of the rebels. They began killing everyone else, looting their possessions, and destroying whatever stood in their way. It became a free for all, a most unfortunate outcome as they lost sight of the more important purpose of their revolution. The forces from Tondo were reportedly checked at Binondo, as the narrow streets were blocked by improvised barricades. The forces from San Juan, meanwhile, were finding it difficult to pour in larger numbers beyond the Santa Mesa area, the defenders finding it quite effective to establish position by the bridges. They had to wait for the armed ship from Taguig to cross the Makati and San Juan areas to blast through the loyalists with its guns. Until then, the expected breakthrough was not yet to arrive.

"Samuel! Samuel!" Ruiz shouted as he fired his pistol, "Hindi tayo pwede magpatuloy ng ganito! Kailangan na natin makuha ang palacio at ideklara ang ating independencia sa mundo!"

"Alam ko 'yon, Juan!" Samuel yelled back after stabbing a soldier with his sabre, "Pero paano mo sila makokontrol? Tayo-tayo na lang ang sumugod sa palacio."

They were referring to the seat of the colonial government, the Palacio del Gobernador, which remained as such because Izquierdo postponed the transfer to an estate by the Pasig River called Malacañang, located outside the city. It was recently renovated to follow a Neoclassical design, a predominant architectural style across Europe since at least the past century. This, however, might also be an indication of the state of affairs in the Philippines. Neoclassicism was mainly derived from archaeological discoveries of Greek and Roman engineering. The current mood in Europe, America, and even in Asian nations such as Japan would be on Victorian architecture and the so-called Gothic Revival which saw inspirations in Medieval edifices.

Since the current captain general was only interim in practice, Ruiz believed seizing key buildings would be more productive to their cause than simply rounding up the high-ranking officials. He recalled how the higher ups of the Catholic Church assumed power in 1719 after the incumbent captain general, Fernando Manuel de Bustillo Bustamante, was assassinated. A similar setup was observable when the British occupied Manila in 1762. Thus, they had to create a scenario wherein none of the pillars abetting Spanish rule in the country would have sufficient room to maneuver. Once occupation was established, the remaining Spanish forces would have no other alternative. They would have to recognize the new administration taking over the reins. As dawn broke, however, the unplanned and the unexpected began to reveal themselves to devastating effect.

Nation Aborted

"En nombre del Rey de España, su Majestad Amadeo, que haya paz!"

The new captain general, Juan Alaminos, arrived in the Philippines earlier than expected aboard a steam-powered ship, the first captain general of the colony to have done so. Alaminos, another veteran of the civil wars in Spain and well awarded for that regard, served as senator in the Peninsula prior to being assigned to the Philippines. Then again, the bemedaled captain general, accompanied by a corps of Spanish soldiers, encountered a troubled archipelago. Manila Bay was crowded by foreign warships, and the capital itself was in flames from all the fighting against Ruiz's revolutionaries. Unable to land on Intramuros itself, however, Alaminos's ship had to avoid the effective range of the city's guns in order to safely disembark. When he thought the colonies must have been more peaceful than the Peninsula, he could have not been more mistaken.

Alaminos could only hope that the Filipinos were still unaware of the constant regime change in Spain and the temporal nature of his appointment, for if they knew of Spanish troubles in their own country, it might weaken the authority he carried and embolden them to continue their struggle. The Philippines, after all, had been recognized for its sense of timeliness in terms of synchronizing their uprisings with international affairs. The moniker "Filipino time" was believed to have been based on this. It was as if every major movement in the Philippines coincided with challenges faced by the Spanish. In addition, since at least 1870, Spain had eight prime ministers, one of them Alaminos's former sponsor, the slain General Juan Prim. The current Spanish monarch was not even from Spain. Amadeo was from the House of Savoy, the royal dynasty of the Kingdom of Italy. It might be prudent to believe that the Spanish government was in a shaky situation.

Meanwhile, the Palacio del Gobernador was swarmed with pro-independence soldiers, many of whom have maintained their discipline in the midst of the chaos. It seemed that the wild looters were not from the professional members of the regiments, but from other malcontents integrated in the revolutionary forces. An assuring thought for the corporal's plans. With all the Spanish officials either killed or detained, Ruiz addressed the victorious Filipino troops, first in a mix of Tagalog and Spanish, and then in English. He was quite aware of the presence of media personnel in the area, most of whom were foreign journalists. Likely out of sense for self-preservation, only one of the local reporters was present. Formerly part of the locally produced El Eco de Filipinas, he continued his career for a little-known Spanish paper after the Cavite Mutiny. With Samuel behind him, the revolutionary leader spoke in a loud voice for all to hear.

"For more than three centuries, we believed that faithfully serving under the wings of the Spanish would one day nurture us to take flight on our own. We could have not been more wrong. It is written, if a child asks for a fish, he shall not be given a snake. Yet when we asked, what have we received? Failed services. Delayed provisions. Dysfunctional reforms. Obsolete principles. Hypocrisy at its finest. Instead of being an ample model to follow, instead of welding us as good citizens, we were corrupted, robbed, belittled, discriminated, disenfranchised. They took our hopes and dreams, crushed them, and buried them with all their false and rotten promises. We are the laughingstock of Asia. We are the sick man of the world. And what else could be done than to cure the illness with medicine? It will be difficult to swallow, yes. It will take time to take effect for sure. But if not today, when will we take it? If not us, who will do it for our sake? We are Filipinos, the children of the nation. We as the heirs of this inheritance know best how to chart the destiny of our nation to the future. Long live Filipinas! Long live Independence! Long live the Revolution! Long live President Burgos!"

As the crowds cheered, leaped, raised their arms, sung hymns, and waved their flags, which in reality were banners composed of red, blue, white, and gold, media personnel softly discussed about Ruiz's speech even as their words were drowned by the noise. They were quick to notice how the revolutionary leader was no more than a corporal, as Ruiz donned his former uniform when he served at Fort San Felipe rather than assume a more imposing appearance. And yet, he was fervently followed by superior officers who clearly outranked him. Had the world turned over? Would colonels and captains be less valuable than corporals nowadays?

"But he mentioned the condemned Burgos," one of the journalists whispered, "That priest was already dead. Why would he involve Burgos in this bloody revolution? He's not the leader, yes?"

"I don't think you understand," the local reporter entered what seemed to be an intellectual rabble, "Pelaez, Gomez, Burgos, Zamora. All the Filipino priests who campaigned for secularization were also part of the movement. Have you forgotten when Burgos dined with Captain General de la Torre here, in this palace, after a demonstration of support for freedoms and liberalism? This is the Spirit of '72."

Another foreign journalist argued, "Hold that thought. Don't you Filipinos claim that Burgos was only implicated? The poor peace-loving priest was yelling his innocence to the very last of his breath. He was never an active party in last year's mutiny, you say, so why invoke his name now? Are they condemning his legacy by using the name in this revolt?"

The journalists continued their bickering as they contemplated how to interpret the ongoing event in their own respective publications. Upon temporarily assuming office in the palace, Ruiz had just received disconcerting news of Alaminos's early arrival. This was within the realm of possibilities, but their forces were spread too thin at this point. Even if the northern and the eastern forces managed to converge in the capital, the new captain general certainly knew where to focus his counteroffensive. If a siege would occur, they would be at a disadvantage.

"What do we do now, Presidente?" Samuel anxiously asked with pistol in hand.

Staring at Lamadrid's sabre, Ruiz calmly replied, "I don't think I'd get used to that name, Samuel. Presidente Ruiz doesn't have a nice ring to it, yes? After all these would be over, I'll gladly support the most deserving to the paramount position. But it must be a republic."

"Surely you can't do that! You're our leader," the engineer objected, "We elected you today. Islas Filipinas needs you."

"Everyone says that in order to escape the responsibility and the accountability," the soldier said, "This country thinks the head is all there is to the body. We all have that notion of a strong man taking care of things like a god. But the head cannot be an arm nor a leg. It can only do so much, yet it cannot do everything. We all have to do our fair share of the work. This time, we have to take down Alaminos and the new corps."

Exiting the palace, Ruiz's hurry was halted by a ragged-looking female child who wandered alone in the troubled landscape. With blood on her hands, it appeared that she was trying to bury some of the people around her. Samuel, however, was quick to tell the child to flee the city immediately. When she looked innocently at the engineer, both men felt that she did not understand what was happening. After motioning to the impatient Samuel to allow him to take his turn in dealing with the issue, the corporal slowly approached her.

"I'm Juan Ruiz. Are you a Filipino, my child?" Ruiz said as he knelt on one knee.

"W-what is a Filipino, señor?" the child queried, "Is it like Bicolano or Cebuano?"

"No, a Filipino is anyone who loves this nation with all might, soul, and heart," he placed his hands on her shoulders.

"Does a nation mean the ones who are with me here, too?"

Ruiz frowned as he thought about the question, "Why, yes…"

"Mm. I guess I'm a Filipino then," she beamed, "Yes, Hiraya is a Filipino."

"Hiraya? That's your name?" Ruiz asked as he handed over a handkerchief.

After receiving it to wipe her face and hands, she answered, "A name my parents gave to me, but they aren't here now. I was told they were on a vacation to the Carolinas. Over the sea. I want to go there someday, then we'll be one happy family."

"Who told you?"

Hiraya pointed to the dead bodies, "They did. Uh, they look under the weather today, so I don't think you can talk to them now."

Samuel then whispered to Ruiz, "They look like workers of an orphanage."

The corporal then smiled at the child, "Why don't you come with us, just for this time? I'm sure they won't mind, yes?"

"No, señor," Hiraya thumped her feet on the ground, "I can't leave them here. They may be harsh in their deeds and their words, but they took care of me."

"We'll go to the Carolinas if you agree," Ruiz said as he extended his hand, "What do you say?"

After a brief pause, the child happily held the corporal's hand and went with them, much to the amazement of Samuel. He believed even a child such as she would have opted to give a stranger's offer more thought. More so, what could have compelled his colleague to literally adopt a child in the middle of fighting the Spanish?

In the face of Alaminos's experienced leadership, compounded by the stellar organization of the troops he commanded, the ragtag elements of the Revolution fighting outside the city were routed quite easily despite offering fierce opposition. Soon enough, it was up to the professionalized core of the revolutionary forces to stem the Spanish counteroffensive. Emerging from the city gate with a few escorts, the recalcitrant Ruiz met the new captain general.

Drawing the sabre and pointing it at Alaminos, the president of the new nation declared, "This is Filipino territory now. You have no business here, Alaminos."

The captain general gave a dry smile, his hands free of any weapon, "That's *General* Alaminos to you, esteemed cabo. I've been in the military even before you were born. Our faction made a new king out of La Gloriosa. What makes you think you can win this?"

"Righteousness and justice will uphold our cause," Ruiz strongly replied, "The Filipino people will triumph not because of the power of arms, but because of the integrity of our ideals."

The proud Alaminos spread his arms, "Madre España is here to care for the Filipinos and indios. The world may be civilizado, but it is cruel tambien. Do you seriously believe you can manage without our firm hand and our reformist spirit?"

"España is the laggard of the world powers! As they scrambled for Africa, you can't even conquer the northern tip of Morocco! As they raced for Asia, you are losing islands to roving adventurers!" the corporal bellowed, the courage he was unable to show Izquierdo welling up in the presence of his successor, "You see all those ships at bay? None of your ships in Manila are powerful enough to match one of them! We will not again be lulled by your false sense of promise and security! Even if we lose our lives here, if we can inspire more courage, if we can inspire more strength for the future, our revolution was not for naught."

Without another word, Alaminos turned around, signaling for the Spanish troops to fire their guns as he calmly walked back to their lines. The sight of the offensive terrified Hiraya, who Ruiz hastily collected to run back to the city with Samuel. This time, it was the turn of the revolutionaries to fire their guns, but the gap in training and discipline were showing. Alaminos was not the only battle-hardened soldier in the new corps. The uniformed personnel he brought from the Peninsula were not similar to the usual quality of troops being sent in recent years. Other than the Cavite Mutiny, local soldiers had not faced a serious challenge in the past two decades, whereas the peninsular troops were quite experienced from the civil wars in Spain. For some reason, it felt like the captain general instinctively knew that he would face trouble in the Philippines. As the Spanish gained positions by the walls, pushing back the revolutionaries and rendering the fortifications' artillery useless, the battle had shifted to melee action.

It became a tactical mistake which Alaminos would later realize. The Filipino troops appeared to be quite skilled with their sabres and bolos. No amount of martial music nor adrenaline fervor would have caused such an organized resistance. It was as if they had become demons in the field, hacking and slashing away with ferocious accuracy. They were a far cry from the malcontents they defeated and dispersed outside the city. At this juncture, the captain general figured they could not allow the southern group, who had just been reinforced by the troops breaking through Binondo, to meet up with the eastern group mainly composed of so-called bandits and tulisanes. Evidently, reports from the Santa Mesa sector affirm that neither jungle nor urban terrain made any difference to their fighting capabilities. One could only speculate how they could tip the tide of the battle, especially as friend and foe were increasingly becoming difficult to identify due to the changing loyalties of the individual participants. With artillery advantage virtually rendered nil, it became a matter of testing the wills of the fighters.

When they saw the captain general and his forces enter Intramuros, the frightened clergy emerged from their hiding and joined the battlefield, hoping the presence of the Cross would bring victory over the infidels who trusted their charms and talismans to protect them, as it had supposedly done in the past centuries. However, their prayers seemed clouded by the billowing smoke from the burning city. The revolutionaries were not intent to give another inch of territory to the Spanish. No other Filipino came close to toppling the colonial regime at the very center. To capitalize on this opportunity would not only be once in a century, but perhaps once in their entire history as a nation. The desire to win. What pushed this would probably differ from every person on the revolution's side, yet they somehow got to unify their hearts for a purpose. They have only been fighting for two days. The burden, however, felt like an eternity to bear.

In an attempt to create enough space for the revolutionaries, Ruiz again rushed to the frontlines with his sabre, "The final secret sword, La Luz del Mundo!"

Samuel jumped for cover as flames engulfed the atmosphere. It resembled a spinning ball of vacuum which absorbed all the energies of its surroundings, the swirling inferno bursting thereafter to disperse the loyalists, some of whom fled out of fear of getting burned. The engineer was startled. It had been a year since the corporal actually fought with them, but it was as if his ability had not dulled. He had even inherited Lamadrid's technique. For someone who had only seen it once, it was a marvel to behold. A wonder to raise revolutionary morale.

"The second secret sword, Apoyo de la Verdad!" Ruiz shouted as he conducted an underhand slash that first struck the ground before a powerful wave created a blazing path in its wake.

When Alaminos saw the forced retreat of those who witnessed the corporal's spirited offensive, he strongly ordered them to stand their ground. The Spanish, however, were not to be swayed by the captain general's words. This made him wonder what else could have spooked his troops, who themselves were experienced warriors with modern weapons and minds of steel. Then again, steel could nonetheless be melted by the relentless fire of a revolutionary's heart.

Detesting the fact that he needed the aid of the Church for the maneuver he had in mind, Alaminos swallowed his pride and asked for the remaining clergy in the area to muster all the sensitive knowledge they could to urgently find revolutionaries who might still be persuaded in the middle of battle. If they could somehow promise them something better than achieving the temporal world, perhaps the subversives would turn their back on the revolution and serve the Lord's kingdom once more by returning to the Spanish fold. Soon enough, they found a viable candidate, who was quick to accept a Remington rifle provided by Alaminos himself and took a high position from one of the abandoned buildings. It turned out to be the Manila Cathedral, which was then being reconstructed after sustaining damage during the 1863 earthquake.

The sniper, however, hesitated as he held his finger over the trigger. The target was there, Juan Ruiz.

However, it was not only that the stealthy corporal difficult to hit as he fought the loyalists with intense vigor and skill, the turncoat was actually having second thoughts about finishing the horrific deed. Would an amnesty for both the body and the soul be sufficient to betray the man who had given the nation a second chance at redemption?

When Ruiz had a chance glance at the cathedral's tower, the sniper suddenly pulled the trigger. An unintentional shot, but it was a successful one. The next thing he saw was the corporal clutching his chest with his free hand, his other hand still stabbing and slashing the loyalists who were encouraged to rush against him after witnessing the seemingly invincible revolutionary weakened by his wound. The sniper, meanwhile, was not celebrating his accomplished mission. Instead, he ran aimlessly from the scene, dropping the rifle that felled the revolutionary leader and forgetting to claim his reward from the Spanish as he went.

For minutes after, Ruiz still fought the Spanish even as blood gushed from his mortal frame. The revolutionaries around him, however, began to slim in numbers. Some fled, while others taken out. Even without fully realizing the gravity of the situation, Hiraya dashed to the city gate, only to find more Spanish troops. This time, they were engaging the mercenaries who were inadequately armed for a spirited charge against the walled city. Sneaking under the bridge and swimming across the hyacinth-filled moat, the child managed to reach rebel lines and asked the nearest revolutionary she could find. None, however, were quite inclined to listen to her crying pleas until she met a man dressed in a bloodstained camisa who only gave the name Raul.

"Bata, anong ginagawa mo sa gitna ng labanan?" the mercenary asked with a bolo still in his hand.

"Tabang, Señor Raul, tabang," she cried, "The man who promised to bring me to my parents is in deep trouble. Please come with me to the city so we can save him."

Raul frowned, mustering what little English he could, "Teka lang. Ah, is this señor a Castila by any chance?"

"He told me his name was Juan Ruiz," she frantically shook him, "People all around called him Presidente. Please señor, help me save him."

The mercenary's eyes widened. He knew who the person was, of course. Ruiz was the one who paid them in full price to join the revolution. Then again, if a mere child was all they could send to request assistance, the situation inside Intramuros must have been dire indeed. Gathering all the mercenaries he could, Raul placed some of the makeshift cannons they brought and fired them against the Spanish guarding the bridge. They were not as devastating as the artillery pieces of the city, nor they were powerful enough to mount a successful siege, but the resulting shock was sufficient to create a crack between enemy lines. A desperate dash had finally allowed elements of the third force to finally set foot on the city, and Raul's anticipation was quite on point.

Isolated by Spanish troops, the mercenaries found Ruiz combatting the loyalists alone. The wounded corporal was flooded with images of his late superior Lamadrid, impeding his sight of the ongoing battle. Was his life flashing in front of him? Had death come to claim his spirit? Raul, however, found it difficult to break through the Spanish trap for the corporal. Their pistols were of no match to the range of the rifles of the Spanish, some of which seemed to be new models. Even as they scavenged the rifles left behind by the slain, they were still at a disadvantage in terms of numbers without support fire from artillery pieces. Just then, a thought struck Hiraya's mind. She suggested the use of smoke to cover their tracks. Following up on this, Raul and his men went to muster all the firecrackers they could find in the city.

Soon enough, Manila was again filled with fireworks, which did not seem to bother the Spanish troops. Alaminos himself laughed at what he perceived as a pathetic attempt to scare their forces. He knew the same trick would not work twice, but the objective this time was not the element of surprise, but the factor of concealment. In the wake of the fireworks display was a blanket of smoke which enveloped the battlefield. Then again, Raul realized the flaw of Hiraya's proposal. While it limited Spanish mobility, theirs were also hindered by the fog-like smoke. In the end, both sides realized they could not advance further considering the situation.

"Sira ulo ka talaga, Raul!" one mercenary bellowed as he slapped Raul's back, "Nakinig ka pa sa bata! Papaano na tayo nito?"

Raul could only scratch his head, strategizing what to do next when the smoke cleared. Beyond their knowledge, however, Hiraya had rushed in the thick of the battle to find Ruiz, who she found was lying on his back, deserted by both loyalists and revolutionaries. The stubborn child, despite her small stature, did her best to drag the unconscious corporal as she earlier did for the orphanage workers. Slowly, she tried to find Raul and the mercenaries, but to no avail. The next best thing, she believed, was to bring him to safety, and that meant taking him out of the city. The imposing walls of Intramuros, while being reclaimed by the mighty Pasig River and the majestic Manila Bay, were still visible in the midst of the smoke. She struggled, she tripped, she rose back up again. Any sane person would probably be wondering why someone would do so much for a person she just met. Then again, such was the enigma of the human mind. Nobody could know its true motive, even the one who possessed it.

As if by some miracle, she was largely being ignored by everyone around her even after exiting the city gate. Soldiers and citizens alike seemed too concerned about themselves. They did not bother noticing a child dragging a human body from ground zero. The next hurdle for her was Puente de Barcas, a temporary pontoon bridge built beside the more impressive yet aging stone bridge Puente Grande which still showed signs of being restored after the 1863 earthquake. The rickety wooden bridge swayed along the river's flow. The movement was compounded by the sheer volume of people either leaving or entering the city, making the bridge quite unstable.

Upon reaching Escolta, which was not even a kilometer away from Intramuros, Hiraya was losing her strength. It was only a matter of time before she collapsed on the cobblestone road. She closed her eyes, yet did not lose hope about Ruiz and his promise to take her to

Carolinas. Perhaps the only regret she ever had was having inadequate power to uphold her side of the deal. Meanwhile, without their courageous and extremely wealthy leader, the revolutionaries failed to maintain their positions. Whatever was left of the organization of the professionalized revolutionaries immediately collapsed. Reigning in their minds and hearts only they would know, but the public was quick to recognize the impending outcome. Some of those who earlier cheered for the revolution changed their banners for the victorious side, while others closed their homes and shops in hopes of avoiding the vengeance of colonial authorities.

Desperate mercenaries were the first to leave the battlefield as they retreated to the provinces, despite being the last to arrive, while the loyalists rounded up all surviving rebel soldiers and their equally disgruntled allies. On the third day, it was all over. The regiments which revolted had been easily pacified upon being informed of the successful defense of Manila, even those far from the capital itself and could have carried on the struggle for a prolonged period. Arms upon arms were surrendered, many of which were in fact Spanish weaponry themselves. Alaminos, however, saw opportunity to better his position in the midst of the debacle he encountered on his first day in office. Blaming the Church and their aversion to the implementation of reforms from Spain on failing the colonial government, the new captain general exaggerated his report to the king, inflating the numbers of those who attacked Manila from the local regiments to over 10,000, while 50,000 more revolted with them in the provinces. It was a nationwide movement, and Alaminos spared no boasts in his role and that of his troops.

This was, of course, based on mere speculation. The guardia civil alone did not exceed 1,000 in the entire colony, while 19,000 more were professionalized soldiers in the colonial armed forces. Only a quarter of these were Spanish officers. The bulk of the military were composed of Filipino recruits. Even if one would double the numbers, it would not even reach the 60,000 revolutionaries which Alaminos claimed. Besides, never had it been in the history of the Philippines that such an immense number of rebels rose up simultaneously, more so from the "loyal" Filipino contingent where the Spanish faith in keeping the islands largely lay. It would be unconscionable for those who govern. Then again, he knew well how the Philippines was regarded back home. Even Cuba, which was smaller to the Philippines in comparison, received a total of 180,000 troops in order to quell an ongoing rebellion there. However, asking reinforcements and resources a fraction of that would need intense compelling power to convince the Peninsula. The captain general could only sit back and be patient with the decision of the Spanish government, dreaming of places and things that would likely be named after him as a result of this great victory for the king he helped ascend the throne.

The Church, meanwhile, griped at the prospect of another reformist taking the helm at the Palacio del Gobernador. He may be different from de la Torre, but God knew what operated in the minds of these soldiers turned governors. For Ruiz to be able to masterfully organize such a widescale rebellion under their noses was the height of humiliation, for who could match the intelligence network of the Church? Even the feared guardia civil who worked on the ground would be outmatched. Yet Alaminos seemed adept at playing this event with his politics. The captain general was even reported to be discussing with the captains of the foreign ships which entered Manila Bay without their knowledge, an act of insubordination in their conservative interpretation. Still, with no sufficient evidence thus far to pin down Alaminos and his actions, the clergy decided to ride with the wave of celebrated triumph and let the storm pass. The Philippines, they believed, was forged by the power of the Cross, and it would be their enduring faith that would keep it under the Spanish crown for centuries to come. The Filipinos would again flock to the refuge of the Church and attribute the victory to the angels' swords and the saints' prayers. Time, however, would tell if their hopes held fast in this world of progress.

As the revolution succumbed to the depths of despair, the aspiring wings of nationalism struck down and broken beyond comprehension. The birth of a nation was aborted. Was it perhaps for the best? A choice of destiny? Who knew when the lofty ideal would eventually be fulfilled? What would it take to achieve the gift of freedom and the dignity of self-governance?

Abondoned Hope

"Ako ang may sala sa kabiguang lubos ng bayan. Ako rin dapat ang magtubos."

Hiding behind the crates collected at the port of Manila, a man deranged pointed a pistol to his head. His shaking hand could not pull the trigger as it felt the urge to preserve oneself, but his mind shouted what must be done. There would be no other recourse to pay for his misdeeds. His was a broken soul beyond any salvation. There would be no other time than now to redeem whatever was left of his honor.

"Viva la Revolucion!" was his last words before a shot was heard.

A Chinese worker dropped his cargo and cursed in Cantonese upon hearing gunfire. He thought it was another attempt at revolution, but when he searched the surroundings, he saw a trail of blood seeping from the crates. He was quick to tell his fellow workers before they all went together to investigate the scene. What laid before their eyes was a lifeless body with a paper attached to it. The words written in red were as follows.

Taksil sa bayan (Betrayer of nation)

Kumitil sa kaibigan (Slayer of friend)

Huwag tularan (Not to be emulated)

"Gowai hai bingo ah?" one of the Chinese workers asked.

The laborer who dropped the cargo, however, managed to recognize the man, "Sakmauji?"

"Bingo ah?"

"Samuel!" said the worker who recognized the dead man as he tried to examine the body, "But why? You're a qiyizhe?"

When their British master saw them lingering at one place, he yelled at the Chinese workers to go back to work. All but one jumped back to action. The only worker who remained immediately proceeded to cover up the scene. After a while, he managed to prepare a plot for Samuel in the Manila Chinese Cemetery. While being buried there was regarded as a disgrace by Spanish and Filipinos alike, the worker believed it was better to be honored in a way than not at all, even though he barely knew the engineer except for the fact that he frequented the port. As a Chinese, he may have not developed an affinity with a Filipino-led revolution, but having faint knowledge of what happened to his fellow revolutionaries, Samuel's grave would be a possible memorial for those who would remember. After all, one culture's villain might be a hero of another. Knowing little about the man, however, left the shaken worker to inscribe on the gravestone the dead revolutionary's name and occupation in Chinese, and the date of his death.

Meanwhile, the foreign ships on Manila Bay began to leave after Alaminos assured that their nationals would be taken care of by the colonial government.

Nonetheless, at the insistence of the consuls, those who opted to leave the Philippines for the time being were allowed to board the available ships. The negotiations with the Germans and the Japanese, however, took longer than expected. Taking in mind the recent deals of the German squadron in Mindanao, as well as the growing German club conveniently disguised as an exclusive casino in Manila, the Spanish were quite adamant to at least have an understanding that Germany recognized their sovereignty in the southern regions of the Philippines, some of which continued to behave independently despite Spanish military victories in the past two decades.

The Japanese, meanwhile, were also suspected by the Spanish especially as translated articles from Japan seem to indicate how hawkish elements advocate *nanshin-ron*, a principle which roughly meant "Southern Advance Doctrine." Their recent claim of Taiwan, which was dangerously close to the Philippines, heightened their awareness of Japanese intentions. While their registered nationals in the colony were not as many as the Germans, the Spanish were quite informed about the presence of Filipino migrants in Japan, and they might ride the wave of Japanese nationalist and imperialist sentiments if that meant overthrowing Spain.

"No, Taisho," the seated Captain Azuchi calmly replied as she met Alaminos in her own corvette, "Our intentions here and in Taiwan are merely to protect the well-being of our people. We seek not to stay nor meddle with the vested interests of the world powers in this region."

Meeting in one of the dining rooms of the Ryukansen, which served sumptuous meals and was richly decorated that one may mistake it as a floating restaurant instead of a warship, the Spanish captain general was accompanied by two civilian officials and two military officers inside. Azuchi, meanwhile, was attended by a lone lieutenant. After contemplating what the Japanese officer said, the similarly seated Alaminos looked around before answering.

"You're right, I understand," he nodded, "If you may be so kind to refrain from mentioning the recent mutiny by few of the local soldiers to your superiors in Tokyo, we shall also be grateful in looking away from Japanese interventions in Formosa. I believe that's a good agreement, no?"

Resting her head on one hand, the captain looked at the captain general, "If I may ask another condition, Taisho."

Alaminos tried to hide his irritation, "I'm certain I can accommodate a request from a fair lady such as yourself."

"A good word for my actions here through your consul in Nihon," she smiled, "would help me vouch for your situation there. I believe you realize what I humbly ask, Your Excellency?"

The captain general rubbed his beard, "I do, but please note that our telegraph line to Yokohama was cut by the rebels. It will take time for us to restore them and communicate with our consul. Would a signed endorsement from myself suffice for your requirement?"

Upon receiving Azuchi's approval, one of Alaminos's civilian officials quickly furnished a letter, which the captain general signed and sealed before handing it over to the Japanese captain. Thereafter, the Spanish left the ship. When it was confirmed that they were nowhere in sight, the furious Azuchi threw the letter to her lieutenant, ordering him to give it back only when needed, and delegating the temporary command of the Ryukansen to him. She then firmly requested to be left alone before dashing down the ship's corridors. At this point, the tears she tried to contain could no longer be stopped from flowing down her porcelain-like cheeks.

Azuchi would only be able to muster the fortitude when she halted at one of the doors. After a deep breath, she opened it, only to find a child dressed in white being fast asleep. Alarmed, she woke up the child and asked her in Japanese. The yawning child could not understand a word, but when she turned to the empty bed beside her, she began to realize what the captain must be yelling about.

"Capitana, please," the child tried to answer, "I know not Japanese, but Señor Tagawa might have an idea."

"Gomen, Hiraya-chan," Azuchi began to calm herself, "Aitsu wa doko ni imasu ka?"

Taking Hiraya by the hand, they began to search the ship. Soon enough, in one of the cabins, they found Tagawa with Richard Haze, the latter fitting what seemed to be a kimono. The lean-bodied Tagawa, meanwhile, had shaved his stubble, and was helping Haze to fit.

While the child snickered, the captain blinked, "Nani de gozaru ka, Haze-san?"

The surprised gentleman did not let his embarrassment show, "Oh, captain. Tagawa here is just helping me try your traditional clothing. I was always in great haste, and I never really had the time to—"

"Kashikomarimashita," Azuchi's amazement was short-lived, "I mean, good sir. We're here because I only found Hiraya-chan in the treatment room. I'm afraid that—"

"What do you mean she's the only one there?" Haze frowned, "Certainly we are at sea. We'd be alerted if someone tries to flee."

Suddenly, a shot was heard from the deck. Everyone in the room rushed out to check, albeit Haze somehow found it difficult to run with his kimono. Soon enough, they found Japanese sailors crowding a part of the ship. Intrigued by the commotion, they squeezed through them and saw a man clad in white pointing a pistol at the sailors, while carrying an unsheathed sword with his other hand. It was the one they were desperately trying to search all this time, Juan Ruiz.

An explanation would be merited at this point. How could the obscure leader of the greatest insurrection yet in Philippine history survive the punitive hammer of Spanish justice? As it was revealed, the meek Tagawa proved to be the missing link in this miraculous rescue. While all were in disarray during the revolution in Manila, the migrant businessman was doing all he could to save his assets in Escolta, which mostly composed of a bazaar selling anything under the sun, literally and figuratively. It was at this point when he saw Hiraya carrying with difficulty the wounded soldier on her back. Seeing that the man bore the Spanish uniform, compounded by his lack of familiarity with the nuances differentiating Filipino and Spanish troops, Tagawa thought that helping the soldier would earn him credit to the colonial government.

He was, however, caught by another wave of events when Imperial Japanese Navy troops under Captain Azuchi's orders scoured up the suburbs to take with them any Japanese national willing to escape the ensuing chaos. The opportunity to go back to Japan overcame Tagawa's desire to continue business in the Philippines, considering the unstable situation of Spanish power in the colony and the discrimination he suffered as a migrant, among others. If he was not mistaken as Chinese, which they call with the supposedly derogatory term *intsik viejo,* that is, roughly translated as "old uncle," he was called *dilao,* or "yellow." Like the Chinese, the Japanese were not accepted too much in the city, forcing them to settle in the suburbs.

Meanwhile, may it be called fate or divine intervention, Ruiz fortunately found himself in the hands of his allies. More so, his life was saved because the sniper's bullet did not penetrate deep enough into his chest. Apparently, a thick notebook in his pocket saved him from mortal damage. It was the notebook he had to write about the travels he had with Haze. Then again, it was quite evident at this juncture that he was not delighted by this outcome.

While still enduring the wounds he took, for the chest bullet was only one of those he sustained throughout the city battle, Ruiz bellowed at the Japanese sailors, "Hidoi!

Zankoku de gozaru! Watashi wa kowareru shikanai! Mu e to kaeru shikanai!"

As the Japanese soldiers wondered how the foreigner could speak their language, Azuchi went on to face the soldier, "Risu Tsuringu! What do you think you're doing? You need rest!"

Haze frowned when he heard what the captain called his valet, but he somehow understood why she chose to speak to him in another language.

"The revolution is dead! I killed it twice over," Ruiz shot an angry look at her as he pointed the gun at his head, "I failed to honor my friends and my country. There is nothing else left to atone for my sins than to take away my pitiful life."

A smiling Tagawa, who knew some English owing to his trade, interjected, "May I be of any assistance?"

Azuchi nudged the businessman and softly told him, "Yameru."

When Haze tried to speak, Ruiz shocked everyone as he pulled the trigger. What was even more surprising for them was the fact that he was still standing. Realizing then how the pistol no longer had any bullets in them, he discarded it, knelt while facing the sea, and held Lamadrid's sabre with both his hands, the tip being directed against his gut. The sympathetic Japanese soldiers did not dare to interrupt the shamed soldier's attempt to salvage his honor. There was one, however, who did not hesitate to try stopping him. It was the child Hiraya.

"Señor," she sadly pleaded as she held his one arm, "You promised to take me to the Carolinas. Would you leave it at that?"

Shoving the forlorn child away, he revealed his true face, "Silence, you impudent child! Don't you take a hint? Being destined for Carolinas meant an appointment with death! I don't have any more obligation to fulfill! I failed miserably! And so, I unveil the first secret sword!"

This outburst, meanwhile, gave time for Haze and Azuchi to leap towards Ruiz, disarming him in the process. Upon their captain's orders, the sailors jumped into action as well to restrain the struggling revolutionary, who believed he could have taken them all anyway as he did against the Spanish, but reality did not reflect his perception. The sword was caught by Tagawa, who occupied himself examining the sabre's features than getting into the fray. After all, despite being stained by battle, it seemed to be of an excellent and unique design which could fetch a price. If he knew that it was capable of slashing fire through ignition, he would probably do all he could to acquire the said weapon.

The captain wept, "Please, this isn't your last stand, Risu. You can still start anew. We can still start anew. The greatest battle is yet to come."

"And you still have a debt to repay me as my valet," Haze sardonically followed, "Do you honestly believe I'd abandon you after you secretly left my service for your own agenda?"

"Alright, alright!" Ruiz shouted in pain, "Just stop crushing my body!"

"You promise this?" Azuchi tightened her grasp of him, "Can I be assured of your word for it?"

"I now understand what Bernardo Carpio felt…," were the final words he was able to utter before passing out due to the pain.

The legend that was Bernardo Carpio transcended the memories of generations of Filipinos. Some say he was a mighty hero, while others claim he was a righteous king. Of course, modern advocates of republicanism would argue if there was ever a benevolent monarch whose powers were absolute. Whatever the details really were, there was no doubt among believers that Carpio was the personification of freedom and peace for all people. During one of his travails, however, the man's strength was tested as he was trapped by a powerful babaylan or shaman. He was placed in between two mountains closing towards each other, while all rescue attempts of his allies were successfully blocked by magic. To this day, it was believed that the hero was still trapped by the mountains located somewhere east of Manila, and whenever he tried to move, earthquakes follow. A simple explanation for seismic activity in an archipelago situated in the Pacific Ring of Fire, but it worked. Meanwhile, Carpio might well remind some Europeans educated in their classical studies of the Greek Atlas, who was condemned to carry the heavens on his shoulders for trying to challenge the gods.

However, the legendary hero carried more than twinkling stars and celestial spheres as his burden in the eyes of the public. Every major earthquake was met with jubilation by the Filipino populace because they were convinced that Carpio was about to set himself free, and then restore his rule by overthrowing the colonizers. The 1863 earthquake in particular made Filipinos quite expectant, for it ravaged the capital itself. Whether it was Carpio's right foot or left arm being freed from the snare, or perhaps he was merely stretching his neck, the promised time of the savior's return was at hand. Then again, the dual defeat in the hands of the Spanish in the past two years dampened these hopes.

Ruiz's comparison of his current situation with Carpio's mythical entrapment between a rock and a hard place did not seem to refer to such depth in ideology. He was perhaps making a joke on himself for he was literally being pressed to submission by Azuchi and her subordinates. Indeed, none of them knew about Bernardo Carpio. Not even the child Hiraya, who for some reason could speak proper English despite being ensconced in a Spanish-controlled orphanage.

As the president for a day awakened in his cabin, he half-expected that everything that happened in the past few days were merely a fleeting dream. That he could try again and improve on his mistakes. Alas, he was snapped back to reality by the presence of his erstwhile master, who held Lamadrid's sabre as he guarded Ruiz. It was no dream, nor a nightmare, but the real world. It all happened, and his pitiful attempt to save his honor was foiled.

With his usual look, Haze spoke first, "You need not to be French with me, John. The good captain already told me everything she knew, and so did the child who helped you. Now then, pray tell what is beyond her knowledge."

Ruiz quietly sat up on the bed, his eyes wandering while catching glimpses of the gentleman who awaited his response. He caused unnecessary delay to Haze's journey, squandering that gains he had through the help of his reformist friends. It probably cost him the entire race. Yet here was the man on a mission trying to confirm a mere servant's cause? What was the point? Surely it would not turn back the flow of time, even as the eventual crossing of the International Date Line would earn him one day, similar to what Fogg earlier miscalculated. More so, if the British gentleman would be known to have taken into service a revolutionary, it would definitely have repercussions on the integrity and the character of the master.

"S-sir, forgive me," he finally had the courage to speak although his gaze averted his master, "but I don't think I have anything else to tell you but this. I've seen the world, but none like you in spirit and in truth. A reformer to the core, an advocate for the nations. If only there were more of you, my nation, my home would have been—"

"If there were more of me," Haze grinned as he interrupted, "it would take the world at least a hundred more years to begin moving towards the future. See, I ought to be lambasting you now. Unleashing my rage over the betrayal and the burden you have placed on my finest hour."

"That you should, sir. Yes, I'm more than willing to accept. Not your forgiveness, but your punishment. I stole from your country, your hardworking and your faithful, of precious resources for my selfish desires. I robbed your chance at winning the world. I can never repay you and your countrymen, sir, so shall I offer the only thing left with me. My life is yours to take, sir."

"Is that so? Do you think it would be enough to placate my enraged soul?" the gentleman rubbed his chin as if in thought, "Very well, here is my charge against you."

The bowing Ruiz closed his eyes, prepared to accept his fate. Perhaps his master would be so understanding as to complete the deed for his salience, and he confirmed this with the sound of his sword being drawn out. All of his late superior's hopes and dreams had been engraved in the sabre of flame. He failed to keep the promise burning, and the Filipino people suffered as a result. How could he even lay his feet on the soil he failed miserably?

It did not go down as he expected, however, as Haze instead used the sword to tap his shoulders as if he was knighting the subdued soldier. This baffled Ruiz, who was quite certain that his master was angered beyond compare for causing irreplaceable damage to his plans. For a while, the two just stared at each other, probably as a way to pierce through the blinders of outward appearances.

Just as when fog began to form on Haze's glasses, Azuchi entered the cabin without warning, "Are you two finished talking? We're about to leave Bashi…"

Witnessing the drawn sword in the gentleman's hands, the captain acted on impulse by throwing herself between the two, "Haze-san, what are you planning to do with that?!"

When Haze explained the situation after putting the sabre back to its sheath, Azuchi calmly replied, "Yes, that's a relief."

With a thin smile, Ruiz made a request, "Please, can you leave me for a while?"

The captain frowned and pointed an accusing finger at him, "You shan't attempt escaping?"

The soldier nodded, "Yes, Your Excellency."

Guiding the gentleman with her, the two left Ruiz alone, Lamadrid's sword also remaining in the room. No longer did the memories of his fallen friends occupy his thoughts. The blame game in his mind stopped. He neither complained to God, nor to the angels, nor even to the devils. In fact, there was nothing at all. His mind blanked after how his master responded to the situation. He gazed at the empty space in front of him. The rocking of the ship did not bother his internalization. Did his second lease at life mean a task yet to be fulfilled? If so, what would it be? A new revolution? Abandoning the hope of a new nation? Make a family and bring joy to them for always? Maybe assisting Haze in his extravagant wager? When the right answer seemed out of his grasp, he wept. It was a powerful emotional display on his part, likened to a dam broken by the water it held. Tears had never welled from his eyes since the Cavite Mutiny, but at that moment, it felt it was the only thing left to do. It was the only thing he could do. The burden proved too heavy for a singular person as himself.

When did Ruiz's crusade against the colonizer begin? During his days as a student, which was interrupted when he was drafted to fight south in the island of Mindanao? When as a child he lost the ones who he considered as family for being accused of supporting bandits marauding the countryside? Was it when he was cheated by businessmen because he had little knowledge of commercial laws? Would his service in Cavite be the final reason behind his dedication to the cause? Perhaps it was as personal as losing his first romantic love due to racial discrimination? He was an unrecognized half-caste after all, an illegitimate hybrid if you would, making him eligible by appearances alone to pass off as anyone but a Filipino.

Meanwhile, the Philippines appeared in the eyes of the world to be doing quite well under the wings of Spanish rule, if one even knew where the Philippines was, despite festering problems in the Peninsula itself and the loss of many of their American colonies. Manila was opened to the world, the economy was booming, especially for foreign merchants, and breakthroughs were being made to connect the archipelago together. Even the hailed modernization of an independent Japan could not hope to match the progress of the Philippines, perceived as the Pearl of the Orient.

Longstanding revolts such as that of Francisco Dagohoy in Bohol, which lasted 85 years, were strategically contained, usually through the utilization of Filipino troops to fight their own people. Independently operating entities further south such as Sulu and Maguindanao were at the receiving end of punitive and relatively successful Spanish campaigns, abetted in no small part by modern equipment and martial discipline developed by years of fighting in the Peninsula and their colonies. Meanwhile, those which were closer to the seat of power such as the Cavite Mutiny were brutally suppressed without question. Conspiracies and similarly serious attempts at regime change were nipped off the bud. Considered too insignificant by the authorities, they would probably never make it in the grand narrative written by the Spanish.

As the troubled soldier kept himself processing what had transpired alone, Haze and Azuchi chatted in the bridge. The British gentleman earlier planned to pass through Yokohama, but never did it cross his mind he would arrive in the archipelago through one of their own warships. Comparable to any corvette which the Europeans could come up with, it was the pride of the new navy Japan was building. To think that a decade ago, the Japanese had no steel warship of their own, and had to even acquire one from the United States for their first, Haze began to ponder how the Asian powers were embracing modernization better than Europeans.

"Don't be so astounded, good sir," the captain firmly rejected the gentleman's assessment, "Nihon's progress now may be greater than Chugoku or Filipinas, but we're far behind because of turncoat loyalists who jumped from the Tokugawa wagon to the Meiji train. Confounded politics."

Haze frowned, "How so?"

"The domains are abolished, the samurai no longer carry their katana, but the old system remains," she explained as she looked at the landless horizon, "For a while, it seemed right for the noble Tennou to accept the shogun's dogs who were ready to accept the new rules. He has an overflowing heart. But as soon as they gained their positions, they began spouting nonsensical policies such as *seikan-ron* and *nanshin-ron*, hoping that causing problems abroad would help strengthen the nation at home. As we speak, millions are still left behind in the countryside, wondering if the Meiji government should mean anything new to them. For all we know, they might be doing so and so in purpose to restore the fallen bakufu."

"I don't really…"

Despite Haze's attempted interruption, she continued, "That failure of a shogun lives more comfortably than an average citizen! Sipping tea, leisurely hunting, and playing with photography as the world burns! Imagine? Even I don't have a camera ready at home, and I'm a captain of the Nihon Kaigun. How about those earning less than myself? If the government stripped him of his assets, where in the known universe would he be getting the money? Not only he, but also many of the worms in the Meiji government who crawled their way to power."

"Uh, Captain…," he tried to place a hand on her shoulder but stopped midway.

She turned to the gentleman, laughing off her embarrassment, "Please forgive me for thinking out loud. You couldn't expect me talking about this at home, won't you agree?"

"I must say," Haze replied with a slight bow, "Your ideas on reforming the Japanese government are indeed commendable. I agree, there is no need for Japan to rush to the world when your own people wallow in lack and poverty. I hope for your success, to you and your emperor, too."

"Imagine," she responded, "if I'm as outspoken as this, yet had no nerves of steel to rebel against the imperial aegis, how about Risu? They did so twice against a world power. Yet, they failed."

The gentleman blinked, "That man is indeed full of mystery. Who would've thought he'd rob the Bank of England to overthrow another colonizer? I now realize why he raised Manila as a stop."

"Will you rat him out?" Azuchi's concerned tone was quite recognizable.

"Of course… not. That'd drag my soul to Scotland Yard. Personally, I'm more intrigued about knowing him better. He'd put the reformists of Europe to shame with his resolve."

She rolled her eyes, "Huh… is that why you took him as your valet? Without doing proper background checks?"

"He's clean. Too clean," he sighed, "Wouldn't you fancy that I hired him without first confirming with the valet services his credentials? I checked, of course, but I suppose this was meant to be. A reformist and a revolutionary taking on the world. What are the odds?"

The captain's words then tinged with utmost sadness, "Haze-san, Risu is in no condition to continue travelling with you. I implore you to please let him go."

Haze frowned, "As we speak, the Russians, the Austrians, the Chinese, the Americans, the British, the Germans, the entire world is after me. I say this not out of conceit, but out of sheer reality. John has to fulfill his role as I have obliged mine. This is his remaining chance to redeem himself. Backing down from that would shed the little honor he had left."

"You lying dog!" she clenched her fist and swung it near his chin, "You just want to be protected by the strongest soldier in this side of the world! I won't let that slide!"

With terror in his eyes, the gentleman nervously looked at the captain, "Please don't mistake my words. If I only wanted protection, I could've hired anybody and left for my next destination."

Slowly retreating, Azuchi realized reason in Haze's actions, "I suppose so… but my stance on this is quite clear. His mission is over. If I were him, there's no need to keep up with the deception."

"Perhaps," he pulled out a handkerchief to wipe his face, "but the decision to keep the story going or not is with him alone. We are but secondary characters in the life of John Ruy."

As the Japanese corvette sailed back to its home waters, the tour of the world hung into balance. After leaving Qing China, the dark horse of the race was nowhere to be found by the global press. The issue grappled not only his rivals, but also the general public and the British government itself. After disappearing with news of an exploding train in Siberia, Haze was again pulling what seemed to be another publicity stunt, this time utilizing a typhoon in East China Sea. Some wondered if Fogg's earlier attempt was just as concerning in the geopolitical sense. Perhaps it was Fogg's electric journey that made such wager a big deal in the first place. The Spanish ship El Sexto Niño arrived in Japan without its celebrated yet controversial passenger. Either the gentleman was a spectacular magnet of disaster, or he had purposely planned to take the world in the palm of his hands. Would it be wise to stall? What if they wait too long to take effective action? All these pressures coming from a rich man's game! Would this be the capitalist world's legacy?

Winter Soldier

"You're an utter disgrace to the Nihon Kaigun. How dare you take action without orders?"

The Japanese Navy Minister, Count Kaishu Katsu, was fluent in English, among other foreign languages, owing to his earlier missions in the United States and Europe. A bearded man of graying hair and receding hairline, one might fail to recognize that Katsu was only a year shy of fifty. An enigmatic personality coming from a minor samurai family, his famous role in negotiating the surrender of Edo (now Tokyo) and the peaceful transition to the new era was a subject of debate to this day. Tokugawa loyalists who somehow clung to power after the Restoration and survived the abolition of the domains viewed him quite unfavorably, believing he was a closet revolutionary who managed to infiltrate the highest circles of the shogunate only to cause its eventual collapse. The reward, it seemed, was the Ministry of the Navy. Meanwhile, his subtle yet determined efforts to "restore" the honor of the shogun appeared hypocritical to them, an act which probably served his personal interests than anything else.

Those who fought for the Restoration from the start, however, also regarded him lowly. Rumored to have kept the "fortunes" of the Tokugawa away from government jurisdiction, even as the new government was strapped of finances to manage a nation coming off from decades-long conflict, it was said Katsu was the primary force behind the enduring affluence of the shogun, who at this time lived the life of a private citizen. Especially those who were envious of his newfound position in the Meiji government, as he was likely the most prominent of former Tokugawa officials to ascend the heights of the Meiji government as well, the revolutionaries thought of packing the navy with people of significance from their own domains in hopes of at least giving Katsu a hard time in managing the said organization.

Nonetheless, there were instances when the minister earned the respect of both sides of the Meiji government, and this was probably one of them. After a heated exchange in their mother tongue, no less in the presence of the Chancellor and the rest of the *Daijo-kan*, most of whom were dressed in overcoats and slacks, the enraged Katsu began to speak at the standing Captain Azuchi in English to make his lambasting more personal. He knew well the captain also understood the said language. For the most part, meanwhile, the Chancellor chose to remain silent as the ministers earlier took turns to voice their respective opinions on the captain's moves in Taiwan and the Philippines. Younger than Katsu, the bemedaled head of government seemed older than he actually was. His trimmed yet slim mustache moved a bit, yet no words came.

It was not Azuchi's first appearance in the Ministry of the Navy in Tokyo, the new capital of Japan after the Meiji Restoration. However, she did notice how the meeting room they met in was made more special considering the presence of the nation's highest council in their premises. If one did not know it was a Japanese ministry, it might be mistaken as a European one. The furniture, the floor, the walls, the windows, the served plates, utensils, and cups, the scale models of ships and ports, even their clothing were visibly European in inspiration. Local architects called the design of new buildings such as the ministry as *Wayou Se'chuu Kenchiku*. That is, the combination of architectural styles. Among the marks that could have distinguished it from any other modern interior setup would include the Japanese flag and the imperial emblem, the revered chrysanthemum of 16 petals.

Before the ministers, Katsu included, could heap more blame on the beleaguered captain, the Chancellor finally broke his silence with a tap on his cup. All eyes shifted on him. Azuchi, meanwhile, was unmoved by the Chancellor's gesture.

"I understand where you're coming from Katsu-dono," the slim-faced Chancellor calmly said, "But have you considered the plum blossom? It may come early in the season, yet its perseverance is beyond compare. Such will to endure could not come from malicious intent. To stand by our principles, we need to demonstrate the virtue of a plum blossom."

"Daijin, what are you trying to convey?" Katsu asked while rubbing his beard.

He looked first at the minister, and then at the captain, before responding, "Respect must be mutual. Azuchi-san may have acted so hastily, but we can't ignore the facts. She saved 20 of our people in Taiwan, and 30 more in

Filipinas during the chaos there. Essentially all the registered nationals in the colony. She also rescued the famed traveler Richard Haze, whose *sekai isshuu* has finally reached our shores. How can we claim to be the successors of imperial posterity, the veritable guide towards national progress, when we can't even defend our own people?"

The navy minister interjected, "Consider the international repercussions, Daijin! An unacceptable act against España is an unacceptable act against Europe. What if we share the same fate as Chugoku when they tried to defy the world powers? Nihon isn't ready to–"

Another mustached official with a high forehead stood up, bowed to the Daijo-kan, and looked at the Chancellor as if silently requesting his permission to speak. Clad in Prussian blue uniform which golden buttons went from neck to waist, the epaulettes suggested he was a general in rank. It turned out to be the new Chief of Police, Toshiyoshi Kawaji. Similar to Katsu and the Chancellor, he also received foreign education, explaining his grasp of other languages.

"Nihon is like family," Kawaji spoke with conviction after the Chancellor's nod, "The government being parents, and the people like children. It is our service to the public to take care of them wherever they are, may it be in Nihon or anywhere else in the world."

"You and your hand-eye philosophy," Katsu scoffed, "Use the police to do that, not the navy. How can you explain to the world when they see a fully-armed warship sailing into their own territory without orders? A declaration of war?"

The police chief slammed the table a couple of times, forming some sort of tune, "All the world powers did the same! Even the Deutsche sent a squadron, and did you see España complain? They were protecting their interests, and we must show the world that if we can do it in Ryukyu, in Taiwan, and in Filipinas, we can do it wherever our loving care is needed."

"Preposterous!" the navy minister raised his empty hands, "The art of handling large masses of people is by enforcing order. We can't have our own soldiers acting out of their own volition."

"But Katsu-dono, consider this," the Chancellor interrupted, "I reprimanded the discontented samurai in Saga not because they disobeyed orders, but because of the wisdom of their actions. Obedience or sacrifice, both required justifications. In my view, while Azuchi-san's move may merit light punishment, we also ought to recognize her courageous act for the nation."

Katsu backed down as the Chancellor, the emperor's trusted man, seemed to have made his decision. And so did Kawaji, who upon taking his seat sensed where the wind was blowing. Signing a document and placing a seal on it, the Chancellor then handed it to the captain. Without reading it in front of the ministers, she immediately bowed and departed from the room.

The navy minister could only shake his head and mutter, "Machigai."

Azuchi, meanwhile, proceeded to the personnel services of the Navy Ministry. It turned out the captain would be transferred from her command of the Ryukansen, albeit the new commission was not mentioned. Effectively, she was suspended from going out to sea on an official capacity. With time in her hands, she left the ministry with a familiar face waiting for her.

"Risu!" the captain in uniform joyfully rushed to hug him, "Are you doing well now?"

Clad in a kimono, and bereft of any weapon for the first time in a while, the former soldier smiled, "Hai, hai. Daijobu de gozaru ka?"

She broke off from her hug and looked away, "Ano desu ne... Ryukansen no daisa dewanai."

Scratching his head, Ruiz chuckled, "What do you expect from pulling that act? I told you I'd come here, right? You didn't have to fetch me. See, you lost your coveted ship."

The pouting captain pulled his ear, dragging him as she walked, "Baka. Hontou baka."

The streets of Tokyo may have no motorized vehicles, but the noise of the nation's largest city was deafening, so much so that one might be unable to guess which was which. Rickshaws were hailed, consumer activity was notably lively, employment generation was everywhere, and the New Year Festival had left its definitive mark as the populace still seemed to be catching up with the fun. Foreigners were also a common sight, attempting to speak Japanese while the locals they talked to replied with their own version of the foreign language. Only a few years back, they would have not been allowed to set foot on virtually anywhere in the country, with the exception of open cities such as Nagasaki in the south. This seclusion was largely the work of the previous shogunate, which feared foreign incursion as a potential trigger to smash the fragile peace the first Tokugawa shogun achieved in 1603. Prior to Tokugawa's ascension, Japan had been in a state of civil war since at least 1467, and perhaps in the eyes of the shogun, various foreigners readily arming and allying with the rival factions did not help.

This closure, however, led the country to be left behind in the wave of globalization. They managed to perfect their craft for most of the Tokugawa regime, yet it was like becoming number one in areas which were fast becoming obsolete. When the shogunate collapsed, it was laid bare to the Japanese how far they had to leap to gain world standard. For one, before they closed, Japan was probably among the first in the world to use ironclad warships, such as the massive *atakebune*. When they reopened, none of their ships was a match to the world's ironclads.

For a newcomer, it was probably unthinkable that the area was then central to a war that engulfed Japan, a conflict that would only be ended by the Meiji Restoration opening up the nation to the world. Unlike the ancient capital of Kyoto, burned almost a decade ago, Tokyo was largely spared from horrific destruction. Since then, the city had accelerated towards modernization. Stone-paved roads and bridges sprouted from the foundations of the former Tokugawa center, laced by gas lamps diligently lighted up by officials maintaining the city. Factories and mills, however, were not as imposing as they would be in any European city as Tokyo remain dominated by its large castles and the surrounding *machiya*, essentially traditional wooden houses with sliding doors and curved tile roofs. It would mostly be government centers, such as the Ministry of the Navy, that would feature influences of European architecture.

Unrest, meanwhile, was also evident in the new city. Demonstrations by hawkish groups called for the retention of swords after the abolition of the domains, as well as the invasion of Korea, a policy known as s*eikan-ron*, and the expansion of Japanese power overseas. They were eventually joined by those who believe action must also be taken in Taiwan and the Philippines, especially as leaked news of Azuchi's little adventure further south excited them. When the two saw the demonstrations when they strolled together, they could only have a giggle.

"They didn't get the eyes and the nose right," Azuchi commented on their illustrations of her.

Ruiz followed her observation, regarding that she was still in Navy uniform as the illustrations portray her, "No wonder they wouldn't recognize you, even if you're right in front of them."

"People would like to believe wars happen in distant waters, bringing back glory and honor beyond compare, and never to place them in harm's way," she remarked like a sage, "But lives are lost in battle. Blood was spilled to baptize the new lands. For our satisfaction, the marching orders of time shall not be bent. Their spirits shall never return to commune among us again."

"I have the eerie feeling you're trying to pique my guilt," he replied.

"Maybe, maybe not," she shrugged, "I suppose this was a blessing in disguise. If I stayed active in the Nihon

Kaigun with public sentiment like this, they might make me the next Saigo Takamori."

"You're not willing to die for the country?" he frowned, "Like the Great Imperialists?"

She stared at him for a while before giving a quick and sweet smile, "A true samurai knows when not to draw the katana."

"Ikuwayo," the captain then dragged Ruiz away from the crowds, her direction seemingly set.

Soon enough, they found themselves in a botanical garden at Shinjuku. Formerly a *gyo-en* or imperial garden managed by a daimyo called Kiyokazu Naito, the Meiji government decided to transform the grounds into a scientific center for agricultural experiments. Within a few years, the garden saw rising schools for farmers, as well as greenhouses to work with different flora. One particular site of Shinjuku Gyo-en caught Azuchi's attention, however, and it was the greenhouse for winter cherry blossoms. A common sight during spring, it would have been near impossible to see them blooming in January. Yet somehow, scientists managed to cultivate them through the amalgamation of genetic applications from within and beyond the country. It made the winter cherry blossoms more durable as well, lasting longer than those blooming in spring.

"You wanted me to see the sakura with me?" he raised an eyebrow, "Can't this wait–?"

"No," she angrily looked at him, her imperious gaze sufficient to melt virtually anyone, "Obviously not. And you know why. Oboeteimasu ka? Sore wa hajimete no ai no tabidachi deshita."

What was in her mind would have been the anniversary of their first meeting, but when the former soldier looked around, his realization was that she was trying to teach him something.

Ruiz took a deep breath as he averted his eyes, "I failed miserably the country, Presidente Burgos, Sargento Lamadrid, and even Hiraya. They entrusted me their vision, their love, but I dimmed the light of reform and liberty. If I also do so for Señor Haze, what kind of man would that make me?"

The captain shifted to a sympathetic face when she tugged his kimono lightly, "It doesn't have to be you, Risu. The Revolution devours its own children. The will of the nation forces its citizens to conform. Do you believe I'd like to see you overtaken by the very cause you fought so hard for?"

"What happened to you?" he frowned, "You of all people should understand!"

Ruiz was convinced that the Meiji Restoration brought forth an explosion of public energy among the Japanese, a process accelerated by the revolutionaries. The rest of the world, across Europe and the Americas, did the impetus of the revolution succeed to create new nations, to grant the dignity of self-governance, to unite the divided peoples under one banner. For the longest time, he had been wondering why the Philippines, of all the world's countries, of all the oppressed peoples, had been deprived of such opportunity.

Her frustration began to emerge, "Then pray tell, how does accompanying Richard Haze accomplish anything? How can you be so cold to these feelings? Has it ever occurred to you that maybe, just maybe, the Revolution was not meant for you to be achieved? It took us more or less 680 years to overthrow the shogun. I believe it won't take Filipinas much longer."

Ruiz finally turned to her, "What are you saying? I didn't make this decision lightly."

Unable to fathom his stubborn behavior, she stomped her feet before meeting his eyes, "Wakarazuya! Irogotohashiannohoka!"

"A-Airi…"

"Risu, it's just," her tone became less angry and more assuring, "Please stay here. With me."

As if suddenly warped in their own universe, the two began to inch closer together. She held his arms while he held her waist. Time felt like slowing down. In the midst of the falling cherry blossoms, which were gracefully carried away as the wind blew, they closed their eyes.

"Gomennasai, futaritomo. Sonna koto wo shite wa ikemasen."

When they opened their eyes to look, it was a stone statue looking at them. They were startled enough to break away from each other. It had slim slits for eyes that seemed like wearing large goggles. The statue had short arms and legs, while having its tiny waist strapped with peculiar clothing. Upon closer examination, however, it was not the statue which spoke, but the person holding it. A scientist in a white lab coat draped over his kimono emerged.

"Nihongo wakaranai ka?" he chuckled, "Eigo de gozaru ka?"

Azuchi sighed, "You know well not to ruin a moment for me. Now you have to compensate."

The scientist feigned ignorance, "Eh? Compensate how?"

"Risu here is about to leave me. Again," she explained, "Would you be so kind to take out your camera and immortalize this memory of us with your experimental sakura?"

"You don't have to do this," Ruiz interrupted, but the scientist already got his camera ready.

In a massive display of affection in front of others, she joyfully reached out for his arm and held it, visibly intent to restrain him by the force of her silky-smooth hand, "Say Airi!"

"A-Airi…?"

After the photograph was taken, and the scientist had left to process the image, the captain went closer to the corporal and brought his forehead to touch hers.

"I forgive you, as I always will," Azuchi closed her eyes, "I'm certain that your friends and colleagues have forgiven you, too. It's time for you to let their spirits go. We have enough trouble in the present life, don't you think so? If you let me, I shall have a prayer of blessing. For us."

There were no words to utter any more for Ruiz. Being in silent agreement, he shut his eyes as well, and soon enough, the captain finished, "In Jesus' name, Amen."

The two parted soon enough, with Ruiz returning to his master's quarters in a Yokohama hotel. In the end, none of Azuchi's attempts affected the former soldier's decision. Whether or not Ruiz had an idea of Haze's insistence to keep him as a valet, there was little else to be done on her part. Initially an act of expediency, the captain had logic on her side when she stood by the rationality of staying in Japan since there was no longer the urgency to maintain a risky façade. At heart, she was deeply worried that Ruiz might lose his life in yet another reckless adventure. Then again, what else could be done? The man's heart was set on satisfying his honor more than fulfilling romantic love. Yes, she admired this aspect of his personality, but as things turned out, she also learned to hate his strong will to do what he could when he knew something could be done within his ability. She decided not to see Ruiz off, staying firm in her conviction.

Upon confirming trickling news of Haze's reappearance in Japan, however, not only were the gentleman's rivals on the move. The Daijo-kan was, to their astonishment, subtly pressured by Her Majesty's government to accord the least possible assistance to Richard Haze. This did not make sense for them, since Haze was a British citizen. Why would the government of the world's largest empire be so invested on his progress? This was also the first official, albeit covert, position of the British government on Haze's journey. Despite being allies with the British and the evidence presented concerning Haze's treatment when he was in Russia and China, the Meiji government was left largely unconvinced. Then again, to avoid offending Britain, Katsu secretly contracted a Korean ship to escort Haze to Hawaii while presenting a cover that they simply left the gentleman to his own devices. The Japanese, too, wanted to leave a mark greater than a mere passport stamp in this historic race. Haze proved the least offensive choice for the Japanese public. Plain was a representation of overreaching business, while Rausch a representation of invasive culture. Haze was a reformer, or at least that was the image he was trying to project to the public. Regardless of his success, he was a fitting poster boy for the modernization of Japan.

Of course, Haze would have wanted a ship that went straight to Mexico, but considering the circumstances, he had to swallow his pride for any transport mode available. It was already Day 32, and none of Ruiz's legendary combat ability would have made it any easier. What his returning valet did recommend, however, was that the Japanese made a good call in having their ship cut the trip instead of making a full journey across the Pacific Ocean. Haze faintly understood the recommendation, since he knew that Spanish ships managed to do so for centuries between China and Mexico via the Philippines. He believed in the folly of cutting the trip until he noticed how the majority Koreans, most of whom were Protestants, began to bicker with the minority Japanese, many of whom were Shinto. The Protestant crew, minimalist in their approach at worship, contrasted with the Shinto crew who set up shrines for almost every god they revere. Not only so, the

Koreans and the Japanese also argued seriously amongst themselves. Apparently, regionalism and factionalism must also be considered in this mysterious play.

The partly ironclad ship, named by its Korean crew as Jangnara, was a dangerous soup waiting to erupt. For the most part, the two factions managed to keep the peace by setting up their own quarters of worship, but the feeble Japanese captain, perhaps the only one of the crew with working knowledge of English, lamented that religion was only one aspect of the conflict. Despite the compromises made, deep-seated resentment was the result of centuries-long history between the two nations. He even wondered in the presence of Haze why it was he who was assigned to lead such a ship. The captain could only guess that it was because of his Buddhist background, potentially making him a good foil between the ship's two factions.

Wary that Jangnara's situation might affect his plans, the gentleman summoned his valet for a private chat, "John, a moment if you will."

After handing over a cup of tea, Ruiz stood in attention, "What's your wish, monsieur?"

Haze raised an eyebrow, "Still faithfully playing the role of a French valet I see."

"I mean, sir, forgive my lapse of judgment."

"No matter," the master said after sipping his tea, "I realize the reason why you advised against a long journey by ship. However, we might have to act before things get out of hand."

"What do you mean, sir?" Ruiz asked as his mind wandered to explore the possible options.

"I'm aware you've been socializing enough with the crew to know what I'm pointing at."

The valet nodded, "I… I think I understand, sir, but how could I do it?"

"You led a nation to revolt," Haze gave an awkward grin, "You know how to handle people of differing temperaments. I figured you can also crack this one, don't you think so?"

"I…," the hesitant Ruiz was surprised at the gentleman's faith on his organizational skills, "If you see this as the best way, I'll do what I can, sir. If I may ask?"

"Go ahead," Haze motioned his free hand.

Ruiz slightly trembled as he voiced his suggestion, "Have you reconsidered going through the United States instead of the Caribbean?"

"I beg your pardon?"

"I just thought America's public transport would be—"

"Hold that thought," the gentleman interrupted, "I'm under the impression that I made it clear right from the start. Going through America is out of the question."

"But sir, Mexico is also America. Basically, the entire continent dividing the Pacific and the Atlantic is still America."

The wide-eyed Haze was not having any more of such wordplay, "Focus on the task I gave."

When the valet departed, Haze shifted his eyeglasses and returned to reading the latest available reports which Ruiz smuggled into the Jangnara to remain informed of events around the world. The gentleman in particular was concerned of his rivals' progress. By the time they reached Hawaii, barring any unexpected delays, it would have been beyond the midpoint of the race's time limit. The advantage he accumulated in hastily traversing Europe and Asia was lost, and he had to readjust his timetables if he hoped to catch up. Since the news would have been dated, Haze had to speculate how far they had gone since. Fortunately for him, the reports were quite detailed in their descriptions, perhaps partly owed to the ego of the other competitors who saw regular updates as a form of psychological warfare.

Jane Plain was distracted by the collapse of American business, which was triggered ultimately by the United States government's passage of the Coinage Act in January. This piece of legislation was meant to end the bimetal nature of minting in the country, shifting the United States to the gold standard. The effects of silver demonetization, combined with the threat of epidemics and the aftershocks of the Civil War that ended in 1865, depressed economic growth especially in rural areas where silver mining was booming. The act also caused a shortage in small change across the nation as coinage of low denomination values became scarce. For a businesswoman who relied heavily on affordable prices for her products, it was a disaster in the making. Thus, she suspended her tour of the world for an indefinite time period to personally deal with what became known as the Crisis of 1873. After all, without her big business supporting the worldwide journey, even the prize of 60,000 pounds would do little for her recovery. Then again, as Plain stayed in America, so did her power to control any movement in the nation through her many connections. It might well be a death trap for the rest of the contestants.

Minerva Rausch, meanwhile, faced unexpected difficulties traversing the Indian subcontinent. It seemed the troubles which delayed Fogg months earlier were still present in the British territory, despite great efforts to finish the Great Indian Peninsula Railway, among other transport modes, since. Unlike Plain, however, Rausch apparently overcame the hurdles and was reportedly moving full speed ahead by sea. After crossing Singapore and Hong Kong, it seemed her trajectory was bound for the United States. The singer's sudden silence upon leaving Hong Kong worried Haze, for while it seemed there was no other way for Plain than to emerge from the American homeland, Rausch had multiple options going forward. What if she was already ahead? Surely the Pacific Ocean was a vast expanse to cover, but it was not impossible either that she secured a ship better in navigation than what was offered by the Japanese government for Haze's service. One could not underestimate the might and the cunning of European nobility.

Pondering on the situation, Haze also considered the possibility that Plain was also using international events such as the Panic of 1873 to her advantage. The prestige of beating Phileas Fogg should have been worth more than anything else in the world. Otherwise, it would have made no sense to embark on the journey in the first place. The supposed obstacles of his rivals gave him no satisfaction as he himself was also detained, by a revolution financed by the robbing of the Bank of England no less, so as to cost him precious time in finishing the act. There was no gain in blaming and finding excuses, he eventually realized. He could only be patient as the Korean ship slowly sailed across the Pacific, the waiting time providing him space to rethink of the reasons why he accepted the challenge. The reasons why he went to rescue a failure of a revolutionary who could have soiled his own reputation. The reasons why he sought reform in the first place. Was the tour of the world an ample platform to attain his personal goals?

Enduring Freedom

"How can I hope to make peace between these groups? I can't speak Korean."

The reintegrated valet Juan Ruiz may have a number of languages under his belt due to the many personalities he assumed during his travels, but he was not the ultimate translator. It had only been a year since he left the Philippines as a result of the Cavite Mutiny, and he was quite convinced of his limited education. He knew for himself that he was not the most learned among the Filipinos. His training was that of a soldier, not a diplomat. Yet at this juncture, he might as well be performing a task similar to that of the world's peacemakers. Lingering on the deck in hopes that the Pacific breeze would refresh his mind, he was approached by a minister clad by trousers and an overcoat. The man whose face had a small cross-shaped scar looked neither Korean nor Japanese. Did the Jangnara take in other foreign passengers?

"Annyeonghaseyo, seonsaengnim. I presume you speak English, witnessing how you travel with an Englishman," the minister took off his hat and bowed.

Ruiz hastily urged him to rise before replying, "Y-yes, but I thought we're the only foreigners aboard this ship–"

"Allow me to introduce myself," the minister interrupted, "Lee Samgyeop, at your service. I'm here on a journey to the United States, which I'm grateful for the Meiji government for their great assistance to the Lord's mission."

The valet could not hide his amazement for the man was visibly Korean, yet was being helped by the Japanese for some reason. Being immersed with Azuchi's distrust of *seikan-ron*, he was somehow convinced that Japan in general viewed Koreans quite unfavorably. As Lee began to narrate with passion his mission to Asia, Ruiz suddenly recalled that the ship they were on was not officially sanctioned, gearing his mind to connect the dots concerning the minister's purpose.

"You might be familiar with the persecution of Christians in Joseon that killed thousands," Lee continued, this time with less enthusiasm, "The crew of this ship were among the survivors, hoping to return someday to the land of their ancestors. I help them in their discipleship journey at the moment. And as for myself, you might have speculated why I assumed a Korean name and is nowhere near Joseon at the moment."

"If I may speak," the valet raised his hands a bit before speaking, "Why are you telling me these?"

The minister was taken aback, then gave a hearty laugh, "Why? Are you not the world-famous traveler Richard Haze? I'm here to make a deal with you in fact."

"Pardon?" the surprised Ruiz tried to find words to dissuade the minister.

Lee continued, "We both know this ship just goes to Hawaii, but if you would permit, I would like to accompany you to the United States. That'd be the big break I sorely needed!"

"Sir, I'm not Richard Haze," the valet firmly stated, "But if you'd prefer—"

"Geojismaljaeng-i!" the minister bellowed, "Get behind thee, archenemy of missions! God Himself has guided me to your presence!"

Ruiz did his best to conceal his disappointment, "Has the Bible also taught that people shouldn't judge according to appearances? My master may not be charismatic as yourself, but he's definitely the honorable man you're searching and a personage with a huge heart."

Lee paused for a while, and then grinned, "I see, I see what's happening. I understand why you need to be covert, Sir Haze. But please, had you no mercy for those who need the Word of God?"

"I'm not Richard Haze," the valet reiterated, this time angrily, "Now, if you shall excuse me."

As Ruiz passed by him, the minister spoke softly and mischievously, "Are you not concerned of Jangnara's crew? As this ship's temporary pastor, I could help you in what you seek to do."

This stopped Ruiz in his tracks, turning around to hear what Lee had to offer in his supposed deal.

"Aha," the smiling minister opened his arms, "You have turned back to the Lord for the great exchange He has provided through His ordained. Let's confirm your repentance."

"Enough about me," the valet was losing his patience, perhaps partly attributable to his master's deadline fast approaching, "You know well how this ship is on the brink of collapse."

"I do," Lee replied with solace, "But wouldn't it have been easier if all of them were Christians instead? Join me—"

"I'd rather pass."

"Why so? Is not the salvation of Christ the most wonderful gift in the world?"

The reluctant Ruiz raised his hands in the air, "If you force them to accept your views, how different would be from your persecutors? Remember, Jesus told His followers that not all would willingly accept the spirit of His message."

"That was during the propagation," the compassionate Lee reasoned, "We're now in the age of tribulation. We're in a race to complete the introduction of the Lord's Gospel and the sanctification of humanity to ultimately witness the glorification of the Coming King, the Conqueror on the White Horse, and the freedom of the saints who faithfully persevered."

"Sir, I hope not to get down in a theological debate," the valet surrendered the argument, "If you could help me keep the peace among the crew, at least until we get to Hawaii, then good."

"Blessed are the peacemakers," the minister remarked.

"But taking you to the United States is another matter, even if we do agree," Ruiz interrupted, "Please understand that we don't plan to cross the North American nation."

Lee's cheery disposition suddenly changed, "Unbelievable... What then shall I do now?"

Despite his underhanded tactics, the minister seemed genuine in his desire to spread the Word of God to the nations, especially if what he narrated about his travails in Korea were true. In addition, considering his supposed connections with the Korean faction of the ship, his aid would be beneficial to his immediate mission of maintaining the cohesion until they reach Hawaii. However, Ruiz had enough of what seemed like side quests which may interfere with their ultimate goal of circumnavigating the world before the time limit expired. He also had to ponder if the minister was all talk, bloating his credentials in expectation of obtaining their favor.

The thrilled valet forwarded an idea that just hit him, "Look, sir. We're in a quandary here. If we don't reach Hawaii safely, then your hopes of going to the United States would be dashed. I do have a proposal for you, but I expect you to be faithful to the plan. Else, all shall fail."

This lightened up the minister's face, "I see reason in your proposition. What do you suggest?"

After striking an agreement with Lee, Ruiz hurried to Haze's cabin. The gentleman was surprised to see the valet when there was no scheduled task for him to fulfill, but he did not let any of his emotions show. Before laying down the papers he had been studying and scribbling on, he motioned for Ruiz to take a seat in front of him.

"I sense you're riding on a wind of change, are you not?" the master then queried as he lightly wiped his eyeglasses.

With eyes gleaming, the valet confidently replied, "I believe so, sir, but first may I ask you this?"

Ruiz detailed the plan he concocted in collaboration with a minister called Samgyeop Lee to reconcile the factions in the ship, at least for a period sufficient for it to complete the trip. The master listened intently, uttering nothing to rebut or to remark about what the valet was saying. He was quick to analyze the implications of the proposal, but it was beyond him that the minister was already attempting to do his role, which would likely make his insights less effective to prevent any repercussions which may come to mind. The valet was not asking for permission, it turned out. What he was asking his master was a way to assist the minister's mission.

"You're asking me if I know someone who could arrange a journey to America?" Haze reiterated the proposition as he placed his eyeglasses back on his face.

"Please, sir," the valet pleaded, "Don't misinterpret this request. I'm not pursuing a course through the United States any longer. Minister Lee was the one who needed this journey."

"I'm pondering how I never met this man before when I went around," the master looked away, his eyes aiming for the little window of the cabin, "Regardless, you're willing to help a man you just met? With little to no assurance that he'd fulfill his part of your plan?"

"If I learned anything, from running a revolution to failing it," Ruiz looked down and smiled, "that would be how kindness isn't earned, it is given."

The British gentleman nodded, "And you don't believe your confidence in me was misplaced?"

"Sir," Ruiz raised his head and looked at the master expectantly, "you're the most wonderful person I've ever met. Your way with relationships was beyond marvelous. If I had a fraction of your spirit, my beloved Filipinas might be a free nation by now."

"What about Miss Azuchi?" Haze laughed, resisting the urge to glance at his valet, "In my opinion, she's by far the one who holds you dearest. Yet here you are, taking me as your role model?"

"The most excellent captain," the valet remarked after a sigh, "reveres her emperor. What she showed in our presence are nothing more than sincere devotion to her duty as a public servant."

He then continued, this time gazing at his master, "But you, sir, have done exemplary things without being compelled by the state or anybody else. You have no nation behind you. No real community to belong. What you unwaveringly carried are your personal convictions."

The cheer on Haze's face faded, "Like any other person, perfection was not my credo. Semper reformanda. There's always room for change."

The gentleman paused, and then turned to Ruiz, "No matter. As your friend, I'll see what I can do in Hawaii. But as your master, I expect that the task would be achieved."

As it turned out, the ploy was working better than expected. Even though Haze was rarely leaving his cabin and barely understood the Japanese or the Korean languages, he carefully observed how the overall dispositions of the crew and their captain changed in almost a fortnight. Was Samgyeop Lee really the great communicator for God he claimed to be? If so, the British gentleman might be the one who would be cornered to keep his half-hearted pledge. Hawaii had robust relations with Britain, while the United States and the other powers were closely watching. This could become an issue since he was intentionally avoiding the British government from influencing his journey. Noting that Japan, already an independent country in the Pacific and potentially capable of international expansion, was persuaded enough to try assisting Haze covertly instead, how much more the smaller Hawaiian Kingdom? In addition, it had been years since he last heard from Hawaii, one of the many places in the world he had never set foot on.

If Manila or Tokyo were to an external observer undoubtedly emerging commercial cities buttressed by the convergence of Asian and European energies, Hawaii appeared to be an island straight from a fairytale. As if maintained by some mystical power, the irresistible touch of modernization was arrested on its tracks in the so-called Jewel of the Pacific. Time itself seemed to slow down in Hawaii as locals and foreigners alike immersed themselves with the gifts of nature with much gaiety, freed from the anxieties of the mundane. The hasty Haze, however, was apparently immune from all these as he immediately met the peculiar minister who kept the peace throughout their journey from Japan as soon as they disembarked from the Jangnara.

"I have heard so much," the British gentleman said after shaking Lee's hand, "Let me take this chance to express my gratitude for your indispensable assistance to my worldwide tour."

"Seonsangnim," the embarrassed minister seemingly losing every inch of his confidence as he was commended by the real Richard Haze, "No need for flattery. I'm merely doing the work of God. As it is written, what we do for others, we also do for the Lord."

The sudden shift in Haze's demeanor, meanwhile, worried Ruiz. Since the gentleman was usually stoic and essentially emotionless, it felt like the world would be ending soon if his master genuinely learned to smile and be merry in the presence of a complete stranger. Perhaps it was the Hawaiian magic? The valet's mind worked on overdrive to rationalize this bizarre phenomenon. He was pulled from his trance when Haze leaned towards him and whispered to hold fast to their bags. When the minister turned around to have a taste of the Hawaiian breeze, Haze tapped Ruiz and ran like the wind. Startled of this development, the valet almost naturally followed the lead without giving any second thought to what just transpired.

The British gentleman, however, did not prove himself to be the most physically fit bloke. His strength failed him after around a kilometer of running, only to realize they ended up in a place called Merchant Street. In contrast with their initial impressions of the island kingdom, it appeared to be a miniature copy of a modern city, compressed to the size of a street. Low-rise buildings made of bricks and stones populated the area, with an ample number of carriages serving the Hawaiians. One particular edifice seemed to have caught the attention of many, which attracted Haze as well, thinking that they could blend in the crowd as they recuperate.

In the midst of the multitude, the two travelers found a man whose sideburns spread out as if electrified, while his mustache was filled by fizz from the alcohol he just chugged down. Since virtually none of the spectators around spoke any English nor any other European language they might recognize, they assumed it was a sort of drinking contest, except that there was no other competitor to consider. More so, the drinker was dressed in a suit that resembled the European than the Hawaiian. They did notice the people yelling words which felt repeated over time, in particular *Ali'i* and *Lunalilo*. Were they perhaps chanting his name?

The center of the spotlight, far from being sober, suddenly rose and approached Haze with a wide smile on his mustachioed face. Taking the British gentleman by the shoulder startled the spectators, who not only were unaware of Haze's personage, but were also worried of what could happen between them. After all, what else would be a natural response to a drunk?

"If it ain't Richard Haze!" the man declared in impeccable English despite his periodic hiccups, "Did Kanaloa snatch you from London?"

Haze fixed his glasses and gave the drunk a handkerchief, "I don't believe we've been acquainted, my good sir?"

This caused the man to give an infectious laugh and wrap a shoulder around Haze. It was when Ruiz decided to separate the two, only to be sternly warned by his master. As the drunk danced around, much to the delight of the people present, the valet prepared himself for a potential plot twist that could have humiliated him in the long run.

With a sigh, the reluctant Haze informed the former soldier, "I recall a chief who in the past visited England as a minister's writer. A young Hawaiian most interested in our implementation of the First Reform Act. Could it be him?"

He then approached the dancing drunk, "How long has it been, Prince Bill?"

Turning around with a cheer, the man replied, "Took you long enough, my friend! Oh, hold on. Sadly, that said title no longer applies to me."

"What do you mean?" Haze tried to keep any expression from revealing itself.

"I'm the King of Hawaii now!" the chief announced with open yet trembling arms, "Ma ka Lokomaika'I o ke Akua, Ke Ali'i o ko Hawai'i Pae 'Aina, William Charles Lunalilo!"

Even after the boisterous crowds literally brought them from Merchant Street to Iolani Palace, the residence of Hawaiian royalty, the shock from the king's announcement still found the two travelers processing what had transpired. Inspired by Renaissance architecture, the palace which flew the Hawaiian flag was no larger than four hectares, a fraction of Hyde Park. It was just as high as some of the buildings in Merchant Street. Even Intramuros in the Philippines, aging as it may have been as a stronghold, was visibly more immense. Nonetheless, it was an ample representation of Hawaii's appeal towards modernity and progress.

"Sacre bleu!" yelled a bearded man who also wore seemingly European clothes, "Qu'est-ce que vous faites?"

"Ah, if it ain't Dr. Trousseau!" the intoxicated king waved at him, still suffering from occasional hiccups, "I'm simply, simply communing with my people, vous comprenez?"

The physician immediately took the king by the shoulder, and in his capacity as a military officer, ordered the palace guards to clear the grounds despite the king's protestations to keep the area open. The doctor only responded in French with stern reminders to reduce the alcohol intake, citing health concerns as he went. However, just before entering the palace, Trousseau's eyes caught Haze and Ruiz being escorted out as well. Realizing that they were not locals, he asked the guards to take the two foreigners with them for interrogation. For hours, they had to wait in a separate room, much to Haze's irritation. In retrospect, could it have been more efficient to have helped the Korean minister than to ditch him? Theoretically, it might have been easier to find an America-bound ship considering the current geopolitical position of Hawaii. With the decline of the galleons traversing the Pacific Ocean, there was little reason for Hawaiians to go to Mexico, which had to deal with sustaining peace after the end of the French Intervention in 1867, and had not been in the best diplomatic side of neighboring United States either since the Mexican-American War nearly three decades prior.

For Haze, it made perfect sense. If he would choose to access America's public transportation system, his rivals could easily postpone his trips as they did against him in France. Then again, being detained in Iolani Palace was not the most ideal position. Precious time that might have been used to search for a ship that went to Mexico was drained, and even if his friend recovered from his drunkenness, the British gentleman was uncertain of the aid he could provide. For that matter, it has been years since they met each other, with virtually no communications to keep them in touch since. Would it be possible that Lunalilo only recognized him out of his delirium? If so, there was nothing to hope from the monarch in his sober state.

As for Ruiz, his attention shifted more to the physician who was recognizably French, yet commanded respect from the Hawaiian guards. The preliminary questioning by the Hawaiians did little to clear the misunderstandings, thanks in no small part to the language barrier. Unlike his master, he was more optimistic about the situation, perhaps taking lessons from Haze's previous encounters in Russia and China.

He firmly believed they could attain the assistance of both the king and his doctor. For the meantime, he took the opportunity to interrogate Haze. Left tied to their chairs by the Hawaiians, the valet wanted to know why his master acted as such concerning Minister Lee's humble request for help.

At first, Haze decided to stay silent, then he gave a brief reply, "I sympathize with the struggle for religious freedom, but using God's name for favors isn't my cup of tea."

Ruiz tried to make a rebuttal, but he realized that respecting his master's opinion would help maintain the fragile amity between them. After all, he endangered Haze's chances of winning his wager, and by continuing to travel with him, the risk of being connected with a foreign revolutionary and the Bank of England's thief was great. An illogical move for someone of Haze's intelligence, and yet there was also a sense of gratefulness in the valet's heart for he believed there was hidden meaning behind the gentleman's subtle attempt to rescue him.

Suddenly, the doors burst open to accommodate the majestic entry of Lunalilo and Trousseau. While the French doctor and the palace guards looked uneasy, the king did not seem to be hostile. He did, however, emanate a more dignified appearance compared to the earlier encounter at Merchant Street. Tension rose from the two travelers as time passed in silence, albeit Haze was relatively better in keeping his emotions in check.

"Visiting gentlemen…," the king finally spoke with outstretched arms, "Welcome to Hawaii! May you forgive my people for treating you harshly."

Ruiz could not believe it, but Haze was quick on the uptake, "Your Grace, you need not be—"

Lunalilo approached the British gentleman and hugged him, "Richard, Bill is alright."

This shocked the Hawaiians, who still viewed indifferently the suspicious foreigners despite the king's orders to untie them. Trousseau, meanwhile, went on to apologize to Ruiz. The doctor was pleasantly baffled when the valet replied in French. Their attention, however, would soon return to the discussion of their masters before the two attendants could have an exchange.

"I understand," Lunalilo's delight dissipated, "I didn't realize Phileas lost his bet so narrowly. If only I have been made aware sooner."

"That's the very reason," Haze followed, "I'm undertaking this race around the world. The cause of reform had been held back in Europe and America, but when we present to them how the rest of the world has progressed, hopefully they see the folly of resting on their coal-fired laurels."

The king placed a hand on the gentleman's shoulder, "My country is fairly incomparable to a world power as yours, but I assure you as long as I'm the king. Every assistance will be provided for your journey. It's high time the world witnessed the prowess of Hawaii, this jewel of freedom and democracy in the center of the Pacific."

This was what Ruiz expected. It was working perfectly, but his internal jubilation ended when Lunalilo frowned upon Haze's decision to skip the United States altogether.

"Are you certain?" the king scratched his sideburns, "With the Spanish Empire virtually demolished in the American continent, there's no viable alternative to the sea transports offered by the United States."

Turning to Trousseau, the British gentleman insisted, "I am. Perhaps our French friend here could offer us another way? Doctor Trousseau, is it not?"

The physician shook his hands to denote his lack of capacity to secure an alternative ship, which somewhat dismayed Ruiz. The valet took the initiative to follow through his master's logic.

"Pardon my intrusion, Your Grace. I did my research on our good doctor," the former soldier declared, "You're not only attending to the king's health. You're also the port physician of Honolulu. Like in Manila, nothing escapes your sight, is there not?"

With everyone's eyes on him, the defeated doctor sighed, "Oui, il y a une part de verite la-dedans."

Lunalilo merely smiled at his physician, "In the Queen's English, if you may."

"Oui, uh, a French ship arrived a few hours earlier than the Korean vessel you're in," Trousseau explained nervously, "They, uh, requested us to process their papers, um, the soonest possible."

Perhaps for the first time since they began their journey, the two travelers looked at each other in spiritual agreement. Haze was the first to speak.

"I have an idea why. Doctor," he calmly said, "have they indicated where they are headed?"

"We tried to investigate, of course," Trousseau responded, attempting to conceal the fact they did little checks on the vessel in the first place since it was registered with France, "We came to the conclusion that they're not aiming for Les Etats-Unis."

While his master contemplated the matter, Ruiz tried to rationalize this revelation, "It won't be welcomed in Mexico. Remember the French intervention? The only logical choice would be Colombia."

This caught the British gentleman's ears, "John, how sure would this conjecture be?"

As if fueled by newfound confidence, the valet expounded like presenting an intangible map, "The former Spanish colonies in America were highly dependent on silver. The boom of silver in the United States outcompeted the mines of Colombia, Peru, and Chile. I can imagine that if they're not after the economic gain, they're looking for something else in the Eastern Pacific."

It was natural for Haze to be interested, albeit he did not express it, but Ruiz was slightly startled when Lunalilo was the one who made a remark.

"A fascinating observation," the king pondered as he took a seat, "I presume part of your reason would be rooted with the Nicaraguan and the Panamanian canal proposals."

"Why, that's quite correct, Your Grace," the valet replied enthusiastically, "When I worked in Peru, there were talks of French engineers planning to replicate the Suez Canal in those areas, more favorably in Colombia's Panama. I suppose your great nation also looked closely at these developments. It would connect the two great oceans of the world!"

While Ruiz expounded on his impromptu presentation, which demonstrated his impressive knowledge of the former Spanish possessions in the continent, Haze was deep in thought. His mind wandered not on the unbuilt canal, but on the prospect of crossing the shorter route through the Colombian isthmus than the one going across Mexican territory. It could certainly be a convenient solution to the issue at hand, but he also considered the faint possibility that a surprise would be in store. A trap by Scotland Yard? His remembrance of the tenacious, if not unfortunate, chase by Detective Fix to apprehend Fogg loomed large at this juncture. Hawaii may be an independent nation, but British influence extended all over the world, even in the middle of the Pacific Ocean. Without giving the prospect a second thought, the master interrupted his valet and spoke to the king with an air of eerie frankness.

"Your Grace, may you be so kind to permit me to see this French ship?" his eyes burned with passion even as his expression remained calm in contrast, "May I also request that you bring with us the most trusted in your army?"

Lunalilo's eyebrows raised, "Are you trying to have a munity against me? Why hand me a risky proposition?"

Haze reached out to the king and replied, "This tour of the world is my legacy for future generations. If I can't be diplomatic about it, get ready to commandeer the ship on the pretext of anything you can come up with your laws. I implore you this not as a friend, but as a brother in continuing reform and enduring freedom."

"Richard," the Hawaiian head of state closed his eyes and sighed, "If you asked me of this as your friend, I'd have complied all the same... Yes, I agree. Semper reformanda."

Haze smiled and gave a nod while Lunalilo called for Trousseau to organize a platoon in accordance to the British gentleman's request. The Hawaiian military was never large, at least in comparison with the standing armies of Asia and Europe, even in the days of unification by Lunalilo's predecessor, King Kamehameha. In addition, Lunalilo's treatment of foreigners earned the distrust of elements in the local armed forces, who valued self-sufficiency and freedom from foreign influence. His appointment of a military rank to his French physician was a case in point. He may be democratically elected, the first of Hawaii's kings to ascend the throne through the ballot box, but it did not mean his popularity was rock solid. In the realm of politics, public opinion changed every fifteen minutes or so.

In accommodating the requests of another foreigner in the presence of his soldiers might be fuel to the flame of discontent among the men in uniform. However, there was no time to ponder on that possibility now. What was offered as an opportunity to him now would be the prestige for his nation. If he could successfully propel Haze's journey from Hawaii, it would reinforce the image he was trying to build for the kingdom's economy. That is, a modern country with world-class harbors. If the Statue of Liberty could say, "Give me your tired, your poor, your huddled masses yearning to breathe free," the Pearl Harbor of the Pacific would respond in kind, "Give me your energetic, your wealthy, your moneyed classes seeking to invest freely."

From the Iolani Palace, they rushed to the harbor aboard carriages. It was a short trip, and behold, the French ship in all its mechanical splendor was before them to witness. Called the Refrain, it could easily pass off as a British ship if basing on the name alone. The crew, however, gave it away with their audible French conversations. When they saw the Hawaiian soldiers, they were somehow spooked and went away. As soon as the king and his entourage reached the ship's entrance, they were met by Refrain's captain. As the uniformed sailor feigned ignorance of the English language, it came to Trousseau's hands to speak with him in their native tongue.

This, however, tested Haze's patience. Even before the physician could translate for his liege, the British gentleman stepped forward and took the captain by the collar.

"Don't play dumb with me," Haze's voice was soft yet threatening, "What master do you serve? Tell him I'm quite commandeering this ship from him."

Ruiz was quick to hold his surprisingly impulsive master by the arms, while the baffled Lunalilo yelled, "Richard, what are you doing?!"

Although the British gentleman did not seem menacing at all from the standpoint of an external observer, the mere pressure he currently exuded caused the captain to sweat profusely, indicating to Haze that he understood the message. The nervous sailor began to consider if the stranger grabbing him could read minds or if he possessed something related to that ability.

Without waiting for a response, Haze dropped the captain and shrugged off Ruiz to proceed further inside the ship. This behavior reminded the valet of what his master did at Warsaw, his guilt in delaying the person who trusted him in this journey resurfacing. None of the people present could stop Haze's aggressive march inside the Refrain, until a voice screeched and echoed in the corridors. The ship's lights flickered. Placed at specific intervals going deeper into the ship, they appeared to be similar to the electric lamps which Ruiz found in Haze's abode, albeit less numerous. The soldier's curiosity was overcome by fright, as was the rest of the crowd. How could a seemingly stable light source behave erratically like that, unless a supernatural power commanded it? The British gentleman halted, yet his expression was unchanged.

"Wohin gehst du?" the deep and terrifying voice was finally intelligible, "Das geht dich nichts an!"

"Ich habe keine Angst," Haze replied as he stood his ground, "Zeige dich!"

Emerging from the shadows was an amused lady, her fan covering her roaring laughter. It was revealed to be Haze's rival, Minerva Rausch, who was more puzzled of the gentleman's German than his actual presence in Hawaii. Not even the ship's crew imagined the greatness of her vocal range until the demonstration at that juncture. They only ever heard her normal speaking voice, which on its own was already angelic to their ears. Clad in a traveling plaid dress, her skirt did not seem as voluminous as those who donned their bustles. Apparently, comfort in movement was prioritized while still keeping up with the fashion style of the times.

Her hair was well-kept and tied as a bun. She was as beautiful as they first saw her in London, the pressures of the worldwide tour unable to break her charm. In comparison, Haze looked like a haggard wreck. Despite Ruiz's best efforts to make him presentable, the gentleman's face betrayed every type of grooming the valet could have done for his master.

Rausch then stepped forward, folding her fan to show her arcane smile, "Fancy meeting you here. I seriously considered you're way ahead of me, taking in mind the rave reports about you."

Haze replied dryly, "I say the same to you, Freiin. I never underestimated the power of the Rausch family. You find me as startled as yourself."

The baroness then looked around, as if to admire the steel structure, "This is Refrain, an all-metal ship that could be ranked among the fastest frigates in any navy in the world. She currently follows my bidding. You don't have the power here."

The adamant gentleman remained silent as she continued, "And yet, I'm certain you're here for a similar reason as mine, correct?"

"Do tell your guess, Freiin."

She went closer to him, near enough to whisper to his ear with a sultry voice, "You're consciously avoiding der Vereinigte Staaten, hmm?"

He looked sharply at her, ignoring the people around who have been mystified by the suddenly secret conversation, "And you're planning to use the Panama Railroad, aren't you?"

Her eyes widened, and then narrowed as she responded, "I misjudged you, Richard Haze."

She established distance from him once more and clapped her hands one time, "You know what? I've got a proposition, if you please."

Everyone in the crowd frowned in confusion, but Haze allowed her to proceed.

"Why don't we…," she said with uncanny yet irresistible cheer, "share the trip?"

This time, Haze was just as baffled as the people with them, "Come again? Did I hear you right?"

The singer nodded with enthusiasm, "I'd be more than happy to accompany you!"

Removing his glasses, Haze could not hide his astonishment, "Who am I to refuse that offer?"

Ruiz suppressed himself from protesting. Nonetheless, he wondered if he understood his master's hasty decision. Halfway around the world, a most sinister collaboration was hatched.

Treaty Trap

"Are you sure about this, my friend? Have you ever heard of the adage, 'Keep your friends close, but your enemies closer?' Someone with that shrill voice is an angel of death!"

As the papers of the travelers were being processed, the King of Hawaii could not help but be anxious about Haze allowing himself be spirited away by his nemesis. After all, if only the British gentleman would not be strict with his self-imposed evasion of the United States, Lunalilo might have easily traced a ship bound for America in minutes. It did not make any sense to him if effectiveness and efficiency were on the line to finish the tour of the world in record time.

Ruiz, meanwhile, attempted to reassess Haze's line of thinking on his own. It dawned on him that his master might have had a reason deeper than his rival being an American, as he had once insisted on taking a route crossing the Philippines. Still, he kept the doubts within himself, considering how Haze did not want to discuss about it beyond logistical matters. Perhaps it was a rationale heavy enough that sharing a ship in the Pacific with an enemy appeared more viable.

"I think you comprehend this well. I'm not only certain, Bill," Haze replied as they gazed at the ocean, "I genuinely believe this is an opportunity I can't afford to waste. Besides, I can pay."

This did not appease Lunalilo's worries, "We've only met again since the Reform Act. You can't be a martyr in the name of gambling. At least let another one of my men to come with you."

The valet looked on as he and the king await the gentleman's response.

"She may have the fastest frigate in the world," Haze sighed, "but I've been assured that the *strongest soldier* is in my service."

Ruiz raised his eyebrows and tried to fix his already prim appearance as the king scanned the valet. Lunalilo's first impression? Haze was likely exaggerating. Then again, he could only trust his friend's judgment at this point. Along with it came his dashed hopes of Hawaii having a greater contribution in Haze's journey. Just before they boarded, Haze tipped Lunalilo about a Korean minister who might still be lingering around and appealed to accommodate him a ship bound for the United States. Soon enough, the Refrain left harbor.

The king stared at the waters until the silhouette of the impressive ship disappeared. From there, he left for Merchant Street and began to indulge himself once more with booze, apparently forgetting Haze's final words with him concerning Samgyeop Lee. As he immersed himself with alcohol while communing with the people, Lunalilo pondered on the pace of modernity and how he might be able to steer his nation moving forward. If a wager such as Haze's caught the imagination of the world, what would come next? Perhaps what could be regarded as novelty, silly, and trivial today would be the next big thing tomorrow. When that day arrives, would Hawaii be ready to assume a leading role? Or would his kingdom be left to deal with the crumbs?

The French frigate, meanwhile, did not disappoint. Even Captain Azuchi would be exhilarated to command such a marvel of engineering. Of all the ships the two travelers ever boarded since leaving London, Refrain topped the list. It braved the Pacific Ocean with marvelous speed, even as it was equipped with heavy guns, attributed to the powerful engine propelling it, as well as the mighty steel hull that could handle the drag. If the Franco-Prussian War had a naval engagement for Refrain to participate in, the German navy might meet more than their match. Then again, if only it would make the ship go faster, it was deprived with some of its original weaponry.

Forty-two days have passed since they left London, but they were making good time. Rausch gave an estimate that instead of the usual 14 days needed to arrive at Acapulco, they would reach Panama in 12 days, even though Panama was farther than Acapulco by more or less 2,500 kilometers. This meant maintaining a cruising velocity of over 30 kilometers an hour, which would probably have a good number of ships in their day screaming at top speeds and still fail to catch up. For his part, Haze was quite happy to see Refrain meeting the expectations of her designers, truly an avant-garde creation, if only the ship was not meant to be used for war.

Extraordinarily, as Ruiz observed, his master did not lock himself in the cabin making plans and writing notes. There was a sudden, significant change with his usual behavior, at least compared to the rest of the time he was travelling, especially when it came to interacting with Rausch. The baroness seemingly had a different dress for each day. It was as if she brought her entire wardrobe with her. As the days passed by, the two rivals began to spend more time together. They played rich peoples' games, discussed highly intellectual concepts, exchanged opinions on highly contentious topics, dined together, and enjoyed the breeze as they walked by the deck. Surely, they still regard each other as enemies?

There came to a time when the valet realized his services were decreasingly being required. Initially, instead of continually surveilling his master like a paranoid, he used the time to gather information and establish rapport among the crew, who still drilled their gunnery and navigation skills despite being involved in a non-military endeavor. He figured that if Rausch had any ill will towards her nemesis, Ruiz could count on newly discovered friendships aboard.

While their 4,000-ton ship, over 90 meters in length, was French in origin, he found that only around half of the crew were French. There was a good mix of other European sailors with them, notably Austrian, considering their current employer hailed from the same country. The captain, who was supposedly named Antoine Bougainville Compton, proved to be a friendly person, although their first encounter was quite hostile to say the least.

"I'm glad," the captain mused as they talked at the bridge, "I can practice my English with a fellow Frenchman. Practique is practice? Did I pronounce correctly?"

"Yes," Ruiz replied with a smile, "So you were saying, Baroness Rausch contracted you from India?"

"Exactement. I believe she came by rail to Calcutta, but we were only present there at the time for routine patrol. Nearby Calcutta was French territory, Changdernagor."

The valet scratched his head, "Why did you agree if you were a navy ship?"

"Non, it wasn't us! I would've fought in Indochine first before agreeing to this private task!" Bougainville colored as he almost jumped from his post, "And yet, French and Austrians are in good terms. Remember Mexico? She only required two telegrams to convince our government to borrow this commissioned ship. I say, Baroness Rausch is dame puissante."

Ruiz could only shrug his shoulders before he shifted their exchange, "You're there when she and my master made the agreement to share the trip. What do you make out of it?"

"Make what out of which?"

"You understand what I mean. Going together. In this journey. On this ship," the valet tried to expound the gist of his question with hand gestures.

The captain rolled his eyes, "I shan't understand the workings of a wealthy person's mind. I know I can be relieved when this contract comes to an end at Panama."

"Still, you do realize that they are competitors in a high-stakes wager? Surely you've heard of it?"

"Non," Bougainville shook his head, "I quit betting years ago. Bad for health."

With the captain seemingly indifferent, Ruiz went on to look for other possible allies in the ship. He could not take away the thought of them being thrown overboard or, if they do land ashore, apprehended eventually by Panamanian authorities for some reason. Unlike the experience at Jangnara, however, he could never be sure about the neutrality of the people aboard Refrain, more so their propensity to be in minimum amiable terms with them. There was also no third party to assist him at this point. As he fulfilled this initiative, which Haze did not sanction in the first place, he wondered if his master had similar fears going on his head.

Before he knew it, they arrived in Panama. The only serious setback was the cook having issues on adding two more mouths to feed. It was Day 54, as Rausch correctly predicted, and less than a month was left in their tight schedule. What was yet to be proven was Haze's initial estimate that they would achieve the circumnavigation in 70 days. As the French frigate departed, and with the baroness alone, Ruiz thought if he was being too cautious over nothing. He at least expected a noblewoman such as her would be accompanied by Austrian attendants, but behold, for all intents and purposes, Rausch demonstrated how she travelled all by herself.

The valet's guard heightened once more when Haze informed him, quite vigorously for once, that they would travel once more with the baroness, this time on the Panama Railroad. Opened in 1855, it was the next best thing to building the proposed canal as far as navigators were concerned. It covered the entire isthmus, connecting the two great oceans of the world via land. While comfort and amenities left much to be desired, visibly maintained below the standards of European trains, the railway nonetheless fulfilled its objectives quite well.

Perhaps one of the reasons behind the unsightly conditions of the line would be overloading. Since Panama's trains ran only every four to eight hours, freighters saw it cost-efficient to put in as much cargo as they could in the cars. Notably, many of these freighters were employed by foreigners. At any rate, it remained as the best bet the travelers had to cross Colombian territory. As Rausch had her papers processed, the two gentlemen went to try finding common ground.

"But monsieur," Ruiz pleaded, "consider the situation. We can't keep on accepting Baroness Rausch's offerings."

Haze placed a hand on his valet's shoulder, "You're right. I only paid the necessary fees for riding on Refrain. I should double the pay for the railway."

"That's not what I mean, monsieur!" the former soldier shoved his master's hand, almost causing Haze to lose his balance, "You're the most suspecting man in Britain. Nay, in the whole of Europe. How can you trust your bitter rival like this? Were you poisoned? Intoxicated?

Blackmailed? Pushed against the corner? Please tell me what happened to satisfy my comprehension."

The British gentleman only looked away as he fixed the position of his eyeglasses, "You'll understand quite soon. I expect highly of you, John."

It left the valet dumbfounded, but as they boarded the train, he realized that his master was beginning to be cryptic again in the midst of the dubious developments between the two competitors. Ruiz contented himself with the observation that Haze still retained his wits, and as the gentleman trusted him, he might as well reciprocate the favor. It proved difficult to maintain this perspective, however, as he continued to see Haze and Rausch doing things together. And seemingly having fun with it. They even sang together in German, much to the pleasure of the audience, who were also foreigners to Panama. Considering that traversing the Panama Railroad would only take a day to finish, he became even more vigilant, without regard any longer of being conspicuous, until Rausch decided to speak about it.

With Ruiz sitting just opposite the two rivals, the baroness turned to him with a thin smile, "May I ask what you're doing… um, was it Johan?"

"John Ruy, at your service, mademoiselle," the valet stood up and responded with a respectful bow, "I'm a valet. I'm here to assist my master whenever he needs."

As Haze kept his lips sealed, Rausch sustained the façade of a gracious noblewoman, "I was wrong about your gentleman. I believed too early the defamatory reports about him, and I have regrettably aided them in the past. No longer."

She then turned her eyes to meet Haze's, "Sir Richard Haze is a man, a handsome man, more advanced in years than yourself, and definitely wiser than most men. Surely you don't think you need to care for someone of his stature?"

"You're too kind, mademoiselle," Ruiz replied as he poured tea in his master's cup, "But, conveying this without the intention to boast, I also have my merits. I'm eternally grateful to Monsieur Haze for recognizing them. My hope is that you would see it as well."

Rausch narrowed her eyes, waiting for the valet to get back to his seat before saying, "Don't misunderstand. It was not my aim to belittle your person. I'm merely demonstrating to you the capabilities of a singular man to face the world. God knows the talents of each person."

She then turned to the indifferent Haze with passionate eyes, "I may be a Freiin, but this was not to say I agree with the ways of the nobility. Richard Haze's spirit as a reformist displayed to me how things can change. Sincerely change. For the better."

"You mean to say," Ruiz frowned, "you entered this race out of your own volition, without being driven by filial piety or national pride or economic prosperity?"

Rausch leaned towards the valet, one of her hands supporting her head, "You're not the dullest knife in the drawer, are you?"

Avoiding her gaze, the former soldier could only give a halfhearted warning, "You can't snare us."

The expressionless Haze could only chuckle in his mind as he witnessed their exchange.

As most of his feared scenarios were being eliminated, the latest one slashed by their relatively safe embarkment from the Panama Railroad, Ruiz began to imagine what might be Rausch's next moves. The obvious choice would be to take a ship once more, but to where? If the baroness shared Haze's aversion to use any options involving the United States, the Caribbean and South America would be the logical destinations.

It was the dawn of a new day. After having Ruiz scour the Panamanian harbor for possible ships to embark on, the two competitors viewed the horizon of the Caribbean Sea. The harbor, which was as recently upgraded as the railway, was not too large nor sophisticated. Yet, they both knew the valet would still take time in accomplishing his task. At first, there was some distance between them, enough for another person to fit in, but then, Rausch slowly inched closer. She had the British gentleman within a centimeter's reach.

"Say, Richard," the singer finally spoke to him, her voice as melodically attractive as ever, and her blue eyes twinkling like the stars, "Would you like us to win this? Together?"

Perhaps ignoring her attempts to be intimate, Haze answered, "Knowing she's a bit behind, I learned Plain used a submarine to avoid detection. Novel submarine technology might be developing, but we can't be too complacent. The invention is around since da Vinci."

"Verzeihung," she tugged him lightly, "I noticed you're deliberately avoiding to respond."

He only took a quick glance at her mesmerizing beauty before turning his look away, "What Phileas found lost him his chance at triumph. I—"

"You can't repeat the same mistake," she interrupted without the jolliness she exhibited earlier, "Is that all I am to you, Richard? A mistake?"

The gentleman's eyes went to all places except to where Rausch was, "You're missing in the uptake, Freiin…"

"Minerva," she quickly returned fire.

Haze frowned, "Beg your pardon?"

"I envy you. The nobility would like to pride themselves as free, but we're truly shackled by the expectations of society. Unlike you, we can never fly and be free, for we're regarded unequally," the baroness did what she could to contain her tears, "It's been two weeks, and you'd still treat me like I'm all high and mighty? I have a name, Richard. The name is Minerva. You can call me that, for we're equals. In the eyes of God or otherwise."

"Alright," the flushed gentleman sighed, "You'd know well, Minerva, that there could only be a single winner in this wager. We can't share the pot. Not by all the will in the world."

"Then I'd let you win!" she insisted, "I don't need the money."

"Unacceptable!" yelled Haze, who for the first time displayed any emotion in a while, "If you won't let this matter go, we should… I, we… We can't go on like this, can we?"

The melancholic baroness blinked, and then shook her head, "Mm, I understand. If you please, I'll take my leave now, Richard. Auf Wiedersehen."

The gentleman turned and took her by the wrist, "Minerva, wait."

She faced him with a smile while placing her other hand over the Haze's, "A gentleman such as yourself should realize it's rude to hold a fair lady's hand, or address her without proper title befitting of her personage. But, only for this time, I grant you forgiveness. This is our treaty."

"Thank you for your kindness. I accept this treaty. I… Ich werde Erfolg haben."

"Not if I get there first," the baroness laughed as she showed the ticket she already booked beforehand, "I fervently hope our paths cross again, gallant torchbearer of reform."

The Austrian lady was long gone, but Haze was still uncertain about how he should process the matter. Even as Ruiz had returned, and brought him to the ship he found suitable for the next leg of their journey, the British gentleman could still feel the warmth of Rausch's assuring hand. He only returned to his senses somewhat when the valet asked where the baroness was.

"Oh, the Freiin left us," Haze coolly informed Ruiz without admitting as to how he gathered such vital information, "She's headed for Portugal."

The valet was relieved that his rival was no longer a threat in the vicinity, but her route towards Portugal made him anxious if he chose the right alternative, "Sir, if I may. Are you sure about taking a route going through Cuba? In case you haven't heard, there's a revolution in the island province right about now."

"Could you provide me a better alternative to bring us to Azores?"

Ruiz decided to take the time to think. He was quite aware that despite rebel efforts in Cuba, Spanish colonial rule might still prove more peaceful relative to the unstable governments in nearby island nations. On the other hand, although he was officially killed in action, he remained a wanted person in Spain for the revolution he sparked in the Philippines. The thought of his master having him arrested in Cuba by revealing that he survived nagged the former soldier, considering how for the past few weeks, Haze did not seem to appreciate as much his inputs concerning the race. Was their temporary amity a ploy of convenience?

He did notice how the British gentleman was not only a gambler, but an extravagant spender. Initially, the valet thought Haze was simply being generous in light of his well-off standing. Then again, his lack of convincing credentials made the public doubtful of his financing sources. Ruiz's paranoia began to cloud the moments he spent together with his master, replacing them with unfounded speculations which further cracked their shaky relations.

The valet began to entertain thoughts of jumping ship without much regard if he would survive the Caribbean Sea, remembering how he fainted at the sight of the Spanish banner. He was, nonetheless, caught by analysis paralysis. They were already at Havana when Day 61 came.

"Will you stop screaming?" Haze nudged as he pored over their papers, "Go find a ship to Azores."

Ruiz's incapacity to emotionally overcome his latest blunder attracted in the harbor one goggled bloke who wore what seemed to be a peculiar aviator's suit, a rarity at the time considering limited air transports. Introducing himself as Saul Kron Worship, he revealed himself a Serbian-American inventor who was experimenting his air assets in Cuba, helping the Spanish in the process. From observation balloons to gliders that could drop bombs on enemy locations, he began to show the two travelers their blueprints. From outward appearances, he immediately thought they were investors in Cuba who he might be able to convince in financing his scientific endeavors. While it somehow eased the valet's outcry earlier, whose mind had been absorbed by technical details, his master was only interested in one thing.

"What do you have to offer us, Mr. Worship?"

The inventor giggled, "Aha! Did you know it would take two weeks before any ship here reaches Azores? If you become my test pilots, you'd be there in half the time! One week, guaranteed, and with less energy spent! Truly eco-friendly! What do you say?"

When he realized it was an experimental venture involving a ship that could fly in the air, Ruiz remarked with conviction, "No! We're not willing!"

Haze, meanwhile, stared intently at the airship blueprint. It seemed to utilize the same conceptual framework as balloons, except that the airships would have used larger envelopes to accommodate the ironclad design of the gondola. It also used helium, an element lighter than air, instead of the conventional way of heating up the air inside the balloon.

One particular detail piqued the British gentleman's interest, "What powers your propellers?"

"Aha!" Worship raised his eyebrows while dragging an airship model featuring the internals of the gondola from his backpack, "I combined two energy sources nearest to infinity. Human power and magnetism!"

The valet found it absurd. How could pedaling feet sustain the velocity of a vehicle weighing thousands of kilograms? His master had a different perspective.

"Astounding invention!" Haze excitedly grabbed the airship model, an emotion Ruiz was baffled to witness, "The workings of your electromagnetic engine! Have you been a disciple of Faraday?"

"Good sir, is this fantasy?" the inventor lifted his goggles, the black circles around his eyes becoming evident, "Who are you really? It's the first time any rich man understood even a little of my life's work!"

While he did not seek to patronize Worship, Ruiz was nonetheless filled by pride for his master, "He's Monsieur Richard Haze. Man. Myth. Legend."

"*The* Richard Haze?" the inventor gaped, marveling at the sight of the person enjoying the examination of his model, "The reformer who would travel the world in 80 days or less?"

The valet shrugged, "To be specific, there were three of them competing for the prize, but–"

Upon immediately taking the model from Haze's hands, Worship pleaded, "Please, Mr. Haze! Let me take you to London aboard one of my airships. I promise you 15 days travel!"

"No. Nine," was the British gentleman's prompt response, "And I seek to leave today. I'm under the impression that you need not to refuel based on your design."

Putting back his goggles over his eyes, Worship took out a notebook and began scribbling furiously, "A challenge? Let's see. If two is better than one, then…"

Before Ruiz could even persuade his master to cease the charade, the inventor completed his calculations, "Prihvatam! Yes, we can, good sir. We'll just have to pedal all day round. But first, I'll have to ask you to sign these liability waivers."

The valet frowned, "What for?"

"Oh, you know," Worship tilted his head, "It's just in case we get injured or perhaps fall to our deaths, Worship and Co. won't have to cover your insurance. How does the survivability rate of 60 percent sound?"

"What do you mean 60 percent?!" Ruiz ripped the waiver to shreds, "That's too slim a margin! Monsieur, please don't sign that!"

The inventor pointed at the ships lingering around Havana Harbor, "Did you know they have half the survivability rate as my airships? Indeed, 30 percent on average! Think of it. When we're up in the air, we can use parachutes or attempt a water landing. The propellers can be repurposed to move the gondola. Where can you land when you're underwater?"

While the two were bantering about the quality of airship travel, Haze had already reviewed the waiver and placed his signature. This triggered the fanatic in Worship.

Holding fast to the signed waiver, he bawled, "I'd keep this forever!"

"Please don't," the British gentleman said, "Now then, let's."

Ruiz turned his head, almost snapping his neck in the process, "Monsieur, you can't be serious!"

There was no more room for negotiations, however, as a carriage was immediately hailed to proceed to Worship's workshop. It turned out to be a farmhouse converted into an inventor's hub, quite far from the Spanish-built city which featured stone buildings and paved roads, with the surrounding fields serving as his area for aerial and other experiments. He then presented twelve men under his employ as his assistants. Most of them did not as enthusiastic as their boss.

"Como esta usted? Soy Ricardo Martinez Chavez," one of them stepped forward and offered his hand, "Cubano. Ayudante del Jefe del Señor Worship."

Haze did not seem to comprehend the head assistant's words, prompting Ruiz to shake Martinez's hand and conversed with him in Spanish. This caused Worship to raise an eyebrow.

"Mr. Ruy, was it?" the inventor approached him after dismissing the assistants, "Your Español is palpable. Aren't you French?"

The valet nervously smiled, "Ah, oui. But I was a migrant worker, you see. Worked in España for a while."

"Hmm," Worship rubbed his goggles as he contemplated on letting the observation slide, "Fair."

"Can we depart now?" Haze interjected, "I'll pedal for your engines if I have to."

"No, good sir. Thank you, but I already arranged for a setup that won't force you to do that."

As they entered the airship, it was revealed to be deprived of any intricate decorations. Worship had the steel structure purely geared for efficiency, making it appear an uncomfortable ride. Perhaps it was a consolation that the gondola was well ventilated. In the bridge, mechanisms which looked like stationary bicycles were carefully placed in symmetric design.

There were eight seats, but Worship explained that they would only need at least four people to achieve the cruising speed sufficient to cover some 7,500 kilometers in nine days. This would mean three shifts of four assistants pedaling for eight hours, with four more continually checking on the airship. The last four would be resting. They would not have to pedal at full capacity for the entire duration, however, owing to the magnetic engine of the airship. He expounded on how the magnets could preserve momentum of energy bursts from the cycling machines, so long as they would not overheat and lose mechanical efficiency in the process.

Taking off proved to be an ordeal for the valet, who had never flown before. Ruiz grasped anything he could, his eyes being everywhere, until he eventually fainted due to his delusions about the innovation. Haze, meanwhile, had flying experience with balloons. This made him more amenable to lighter-than-air flight than the former soldier, lowering his hopes of having Ruiz pedal the mechanism in the extraordinary case one of the assistants fail during the journey.

He was more occupied in taking a gamble with an experimental airship, which Worship dubbed as *Black George* even though it was painted white, to win the wager. The British gentleman realized he would again have to deal with a virtual information blackout for the next nine days or so, since the airship was not designed to have stopovers. He would like to believe, at least in theory, that he was ahead as Rausch would like to tell him. However, it was no time to be cajoled. Each day that passed, he believed he already lost chances to bring home the honor.

As Haze pondered on the operational mistakes he would have to compensate with his present consequences, his true rival Jane Plain was convinced she was the one making incredible progress. By spinning news that she was behind in the race, an image reinforced by her staying in the United States for a while to manage her assets, the American businesswoman hastily crossed the Pacific, concealing her real location after leaving the mainland through a concerted media campaign to confuse reporters and aggregators alike. As much as the gentleman would take information from available updates with reservation, Plain made it nearly impossible even for the keenest observers to extrapolate her genuine whereabouts. Alas, eighteen days remain.

Ascendant Celebrity

"Why would you leave your operations in Cuba? Isn't war a more profitable venture for you?"

The seemingly acrophobic Ruiz somewhat recovered his balance after waking up, trying to keep his mind off the flying business by conversing with the airship inventor. Black George was massive, even in experimental standards, measuring over 120 meters in length and 12 meters in diameter. Worship, however, stuck with using helium instead of the lighter element hydrogen. Hovering at around 300 meters from sea level, they were cruising at 30 kilometers an hour, an unbelievable feat for eight pedaling feet to accomplish regardless of the electromagnetic engine.

"I'm not mincing words if I say yes, war is the mother of invention," the inventor said as he navigated the ship with the help of his assistants, "Ceballos was quite perceptive of my assets. That's all there is. Not profit nor sentimentality made much difference. Science reigns supreme."

"The Cubanos fight for a cause," the valet frowned, his revolutionary spirit sparked once more, "Have you realized you've unnecessarily become a stumbling block to their freedoms?"

"If the Cubans hired me to make them weapons of destruction," Worship shrugged, "I'd also take them up for the offer. Knowledge, information, data, science. These shouldn't be bound by any ideology if they're to be useful to everyone who needs them."

"And today," the inventor continued as Ruiz searched for anything he could rebut, "Mr. Haze is the one who needs science, to win his wager. His payment of 10,000 pounds? I admit, I can't believe he'd spend for us as much as he initially betted. I would've helped him for less."

They both shift their gaze to the British gentleman, who in the other side of the bridge was busy in writing and thinking to himself. Haze was positioned there for the gas lights were somehow shining the brightest on that side. The valet regretted that he ever doubted his master, who indirectly saved him from death in the Philippines, and reaccepted him in service even if it risked his own reputation, while the inventor was bent on making the voyage a success despite the glaring lack of test flights for his airships. The technology, after all, was developing to this day.

The week passed on like a watch in midnight, the monotonous and strenuous exchange of assistants cycling, resting, and checking the airship taking its toll not only on the crew themselves, but also on their employers. Never has it been in the history of humanity had such a long-distance trip up in the air was attempted, and while there were minor setbacks easily remedied along the way, the prospects of crossing the entire Atlantic Ocean became less credible for some who were on board. Head Assistant Martinez certainly noticed the changing mood.

"Señor Ruy?" he asked Ruiz as they met in the empty dining area during his break, "Un momento, por favor."

"S-si," the valet replied upon taking his seat, "Que quieres usted?"

Martinez cleared his throat, "My English is limited, but I try so others won't understand. Claro?"

After Ruiz nodding in acknowledgement, the head assistant went on, "The crew growing restless. Hard to believe we're making progress when all we see are the blue seas."

"Martinez," the former soldier reached out a hand, "You can't mutiny in this ship. It would be in your best interests to keep serving your master now, and then rethink your career options after."

"No, Señor," Martinez shook his head, his bangs swaying along as he did, "Not about I. My worry goes to my fellow assistants. Maybe we work together? Señor Worship is man of vision. I believe his work in ciencias. I want to be buen cientifico, but some don't truly share this passion."

"Of course, I'll help," Ruiz placed a hand on his chest, "Let me know how to keep them at peace."

"Muchas gracias, Señor!" a wide smile lightened up the head assistant's face, "Muy bueno!"

In the next two days, Ruiz and Martinez did what they could to entertain the assistants, from fascinating stories the world over to fantastic legends which continue to persist to this day. It was a wonderland packaged as an in-flight program. Who knew the valet could perform party tricks right off the bat, without the benefit of proper magician training? Even his master was surprised to see that while their journey was about to finish, he had a few more aces left in his sleeves. Except that it was not yet ending. London was not yet in sight, nor any silhouette resembling the British coast. Day 70 had passed, but no landing had been performed.

This caused the fuming Haze to confront Worship and the non-pedaling assistants. Never had Ruiz seen his master as furious as he was at this moment, evidently incomparable to his outbursts in Warsaw and in Hawaii. The gentleman was like a dormant volcano erupting, and there was no stopping him in making a mess out of the delicate airship.

"Are you trying to make a fool out of me?!" Haze punched the inventor on the face, causing the goggles to break upon impact, "Have I not been generous enough?! We're both making calculations! How could we mistake anything—"

The valet held his master with great might to restrain his movement, but he was being overpowered by a bloke who was supposedly weaker than him in the physical sense. Haze did not mind when his glasses fell. He was relentless in assaulting everyone.

Worship, who was thrown to the ground by Haze's attack, attempted to keep a positive attitude, "Good sir, we're still on track to land within the limit of 80 days. Isn't that what matters now?"

The inventor's assistants began to back up their employer, the words they say drowning each other in the process. Since they spoke a myriad of languages, Haze felt he was in the Tower of Babel. Without listening to any of their pleas, the British gentleman further stressed his views.

"I want all eight pedals operated! I'll pedal if I have to! I accept no excuses! I don't care if the engine overheats! We have to reach London before anyone else does!"

Reaching out for his sextant, Worship frantically analyzed why they were not yet in London skies. It was then he found out that they unintentionally overshot their destination. The airship was already flying over the North Sea, bound for the Netherlands instead of England. In retrospect, the inventor almost kept his pledge of reaching Britain in nine days, but they missed the part of actually landing out of their haste to make it in time. This fact calmed Haze a bit, settling for a seat in the bridge while requesting Ruiz to prepare him a cup of tea.

The inventor and his assistants, meanwhile, profusely apologized to their latest client. They repaid his trust with faulty navigation and operational errors. As a compromise, Worship had six of his assistants pedal to speed up the final stretch of their journey, which was involuntarily extended by a few hundred kilometers because of their incompetence. Then again, Ruiz sympathized with Worship and his team. Not only was it their first time continuously flying the distance a fifth of the world's circumference, considering airship trials elsewhere would be satisfied covering less than that, they were also working on short notice.

Leaving the gentleman alone, the valet assured the inventor, "Please don't take his anger to heart. I'm quite sure deep inside, he's sincerely appreciative of your innovative efforts."

Worship chuckled as he put on a new pair of goggles, "We don't. He's justified anyhow. Man's desire for victory is insatiable. Achieving one peak would lead to pursuing another. And yet, peace comes when you realize all events constitute bits and chunks of data in an ocean of information."

"What does it have to do with anything?"

The inventor left without responding, convinced that Haze was likely acting more than mere impulse when he lambasted their performance. For a usually calm personality to act up, there must be reason behind his action, unless of course it was a sort of disorder. Then again, with London so close, there was no time for him to consider other possibilities. Psychology, after all, was not his line of expertise. Worship had to focus on his specialization to fulfill his part of the contract if they sought to land safely, and to eventually add the project to his resume.

Fortunately for them, increasing his workforce to six did not cause the electromagnetic engine to fail. His design had outdone itself, and on the seventy-second day, March 14, they saw the target city in all its imperial splendor. To see it from such a height made London even more impressive. Edifices made of stone sprawled out in all directions. From the Tower of London to the River Thames, it was a familiar sight, like a mother warmly embracing her child. To be home again after nearly three months produced a relaxing feel for Haze. Upon looking down, he witnessed violent crowds forming in the streets.

"The ghost of Napoleon returns!" one of the frenzied citizens shouted, referring to the past hysteria from alleged plans of French Emperor Napoleon Bonaparte to use airships in his invasion of Britain.

"The sky is falling on our heads!" wailed another citizen carrying a pitchfork while covering his head with a metal pan.

"The end of the world is nigh! Repent and be baptized!" yelled yet another while waving a Bible.

More level-headed Londoners, meanwhile, welcomed the airship. Raising British banners and making noise with whatever they could find, they fervently hoped it was Richard Haze making a dramatically triumphant return to his city. The warm reception for the gentleman were not only confined with those who betted on him, but also to those who followed his progress. Slowly but surely, he gained believers, from the Warsaw incident to the explosion of the Trans-Siberian, from the disappearance in the East China Sea to the crossing of the Pacific. The dark horse of the race, whose great vehicle hovered over the city, had become an instant celebrity. Soon enough, the news of his impending homecoming reached Her Majesty's Government.

"By hiring this massive airship without making any bank withdrawals," Scotland Yard's commissioner accused while in a meeting at Downing Street, "Richard Haze is beyond reasonable doubt the man who stole from the Bank of England! Where else could he have gotten the wealth to finance this monstrosity?"

The Prime Minister leaned on his chair as he looked out the window, "We've been mistaken before in pinning the blame on Phileas Fogg. We've been wrong in slashing the pensions of our officers. We can't risk another blunder."

"We already antagonized Haze after covertly warning the governments of the United States, Hawaii, and Japan about him," the Foreign Secretary spoke while rubbing the chin, "His *misadventures* made us look bad in the international community. What do we have to lose?"

The Home Secretary stood up, "We have to consider the security threat brought about by this mysterious airship. If we can't enforce traffic rules in all possible routes, are we condoning the utter disregard for safety in our sacred skies?"

"In addition, based on our analyses," the commissioner asserted, "Haze purposely avoided all of Her Majesty's territories! We all know the British transport system is the most efficient in the world. Why take such pains for a game if he had nothing to hide from our global empire?"

"We have to decide now," the Home Secretary seconded, "Would we let a dishonorable man claim the moral ascendancy for winning this novelty of a gamble?"

In the outskirts of London, there was another person of significance overly distressed by the looming presence of the airship. It was Plain, who was already in a carriage hurtling to the city. She opened the door to check the flying vehicle herself, while loudly pressuring her coach driver to go faster. Fortunately for her, there was a hindrance to Haze's plans.

"They're shooting at us!" Ruiz called out to the crew, "How can we land the ship?"

Worship grabbed his binoculars to pinpoint the source of gunfire. They were coming from the frightened Metropolitan Police, who thought the airship was attempting to incite riots in the capital. Supporting this view was the fact that people have gathered in Hyde Park almost immediately, overwhelming their forces. While they were acting without orders, it persuaded the British gentleman that the government still suspected him after being away for so long.

"I don't fear they'd pierce the gondola," the inventor replied, "It's our balloon full of helium that I'm concerned about. A single leak and we lose much control of the airship. We'll have to increase our altitude to avoid their effective range."

"There's no more time to waste," Haze interjected, "We'll have to land on Hyde Park now."

"What are you saying, monsieur?" the valet gulped, loosening his collar as he asked.

Looking at the gentleman's eyes, Worship got a gist of what Haze was suggesting, "Good sir, you most certainly can't use parachutes. A few holes and gravity would get the best of you."

"Señor, por favor," Martinez raised his hand to attract their attention, "Maybe there's a way. Remember the emergency landing system you asked to install? Black George has some."

The inventor removed his goggles out of disbelief, "I'd let your unwarranted initiative pass for now. You're just about to save this journey, you meddling maverick!"

Without giving it a second thought, he gave orders to his assistants to undertake Project A. The short-term effect was ascending the airship to a height of around 600 meters, straining the limits of the vehicle. On the bright side, they were mostly out of the range of the guns. From there, maneuvers were done to crank out wings from both sides of the gondola. Simultaneously, long metal bars resembling sled bases emerged from the bottom. Nuts and bolts felt like coming off, and they sure sounded like it, but the two travelers could only maximize their confidence that the so-called "harbingers of death" of the Cuban Revolution were making the right call.

The American businesswoman was already in the vicinity of Hyde Park when she saw the airship gaining altitude. Her path to victory, however, was hampered by ensuing traffic. A sea of people was out to harass or to cheer for the flying machine. Throwing her payment to the driver, the affluent lady in jumpers and trousers leaped out of the carriage with her bag to make a run for it. When the British realized who she was, they turned against her, and intentionally blocked her way as much as possible. With hometown advantage seemingly played against her, she aimed for alternative routes where there would be less people to encounter. There was no room for panic. As long as she made use of aisles and narrow passages, she could certainly find a way out.

"Halt! You shan't pass!" a lady in uniform brandished a sword to stop Plain on her tracks, "Where do you think you're headed?"

This incensed the businesswoman, who took on a fighting pose, "Make way! Don't you recognize who I am? You're way over your head!"

The unknown lady grinned, and then threw another sword for Plain, "You're Jane Plain, and you seek to win this wager, yes?"

Upon perfectly catching the sheathed weapon, the puzzled American asked, "What's the meaning of this? Who are you?"

"You'll know in due time. For now, let's cut our way through, shall we?"

With a determined war cry, the two ladies slashed the sheathed swords away like mad. This scared and dispersed some crowds, creating sufficient space for them to dash for Hyde Park. Then again, there was another reason why the people who gathered in Hyde Park were running for their lives. Worship's gondola had finally stretched its wings and detached from the envelope. The steel bird was projected to dive on the grassy field in approximately 12 seconds.

Unlike a New Year's countdown, however, there seemed to be no time to count at all. As it crashed, the landing gear held its own, but had scraped the field like a flesh wound. Everyone else returned to surround the vehicle, comparable to ants gathering around food. Haze's supporters purposely shielded the travelers from his detractors, and even from the police, albeit they were equipped with nothing more than what they have with them, such as bags, umbrellas, books, sticks, and banners. Little by little, a clear path to the makeshift stage was made. Taking their bags with him, Ruiz urged his master to go on ahead to claim his winnings.

Excitement was at fever pitch. The rush on his veins empowered the British gentleman to sprint like he had never sprinted before. Every second that passed, each step made, in the midst of the rumbustious scene weighed heavily, as if he they were chains that needed to be broken.

"Not so fast, Mr. Haze!" declared Plain, who successfully made a somersault in front of him, "The sun today sets on the British Empire, for it shall shine on the land of the free and the brave!"

Following her with a similarly spectacular jump, featuring a mid-air spin sufficient to shame acrobats and gymnasts alike, turned out to be a person well known to them.

"Captain Azuchi?!" the valet just behind Haze was shocked to the point of dropping their bags.

"That's Captain Azuchi *Airi* to you, thank you very much!" the dignified Japanese lady shot back, showing her katana at hand.

"Why are you doing this, dear captain?" the exhausted Haze tried to recover his breath as the loss of energy began to set in.

With both women drawing their swords, the two proclaimed in unison, "Fortis Fortuna adiuvat!"

"Oh, there'd be fighting? That's not in our contract," Worship whistled as he adjusted his goggles and prepared to fall back, "Please allow us to take our leave. Let's proceed, my assistants."

The synchronous offensive by Plain and Azuchi would likely make an external observer believe they had been working together for the longest time, but in reality, they only met minutes ago. As Haze proved incapable of engaging in combat with his tired state, Ruiz quickly took out Lamadrid's sabre to defend. This caused a change in expression for the Japanese captain, who immediately warned the American businesswoman about the valet's legendary weapon.

"The longer you stay here," Azuchi's valiant façade concealed her worry of Ruiz, "The better the chances for Scotland Yard to arrest you. If you let Plain-san win this, you can still escape the authorities. Your choice lies before you!"

Without taking a specific stance, Ruiz confidently walked towards them, as if he was protected by an air of invincibility, "Monsieur Haze needs to win this wager. I know not why you're helping a woman with nothing to lose, but I'll certainly make a path here and now."

In one fluid strike, he disarmed Plain. Her sword spun out of her hand in a split second. Azuchi saw a slight opening as she darted towards him with her katana. Although Ruiz was able to block the powerful first attack, the captain followed with a relentless flurry against him. The Japanese lady believed she was gaining the initiative. Surely, he had not yet recovered fully from the injuries of the past revolution, more so since he had to recuperate while travelling the world on a strict deadline. The American lady, meanwhile, drew out a pistol. Despite her training, she was having difficulty aiming as Ruiz was keeping the duel within his effective reach. If either one of the fighters back off, Plain would likely have an opportunity to fire against Haze or Ruiz.

"John, she has a gun!" his master cautioned as he attempted to find a path to the stage.

This prompted the valet to temporarily gain distance and conduct his fourth secret sword, "Columna de Fuego!"

He used a strong leap to cover the use of the igniter, after which he hacked downwards to form what would appear like a pillar of flames. This enticed everyone in the scene, all except for Plain. As she saw the sudden blowout, the American fired the trigger without much thinking. She had no idea if she hit anyone or anything. Yet after the flames have subsided, she collapsed on her knees, and released the pistol from her hands.

The ruckus around them declined almost immediately as they witnessed the horrifying scene. In the midst of the charred field was Ruiz holding the bloodied captain on his arms. For a while, differences between Haze's supporters and opponents diminished. Some began to call for medical assistance, while others prayed on the spot. The police, meanwhile, had become ambivalent on whether arresting Haze, for whatever reason they could come up at that moment, or keeping public order, which they believe Haze helped destabilize, should take top priority. If danger to human life would be sufficient to unite all sectors of society, then it only went to demonstrate how nothing else could hope to come close. Not money nor power. Not fame nor prestige. Not law nor organization. Without life, how else could everything in this temporal world be optimized?

With victory so near, would it be deemed wise to forge on and take the prize?

Captive Philosophy

"Go, Sir Haze! Please go! I'll handle it all from here!"

Hugging tightly the Japanese captain, Ruiz made it clear to his master that it would be as far as he could go in this race. Haze, for his part, knew none of his sympathy could help save a human life. Also, with his other rival petrified, it was a perfect opportunity to take the stage. He slowly stood up. Dragging his feet, he begrudgingly went forward, but his energy to proceed was lost. When the crowds noticed how reluctant he was to finish the circumnavigation of the world, they raised him up and passed him on towards the stage despite his objections.

"Sawagashi…," Azuchi softly spoke as she woke up and found blood on her hands.

The teary-eyed valet smiled as he gently stroked her hair, "You're awake? Don't fret. A doctor will arrive at the soonest."

Noticing how contorted his face had become in attempting to placate her, she touched his cheek, "As much as you hated lengthy dialogues in theaters, this isn't the melodramatic finale you expected?"

"Please don't say it like that," he pleaded, "You're stronger than a speeding bullet, but you should've not sacrificed for my sake."

"Forgive me," she buried her face on his coat, "I feared you won't return to me, if Haze-san won… I'm here for a study mission… I suppose, I won't have anything to report…"

"Airi, that's not true–"

"My consolation, Risu… That is, you're here with me."

"Make way! The ultimate doctor has arrived in the scene!" Worship announced as he escorted a physician to where the shot captain was.

First aid was conducted. They thought it better for the meantime since the sheer amount of traffic around Hyde Park might make it less plausible to try transporting the wounded to the nearest hospital. It might have been easier if an air transport was available, but Black George's envelope was no more. As this was ongoing, the inventor turned his attention to Haze's dejected rival.

Offering his hand after taking the pistol away, he assured her, "Come here, I won't bite."

This snapped her back to reality, her eyes still on the captain who helped her, "Is this the American dream? I believed in my advantage. The submarine decoy worked. My log says it's only Day 71. No other mind in the world knew where I was. How could he arrive here earlier than me?"

"When we're captive of our own philosophies," he replied while emptying the gun of ammunition, "we're like horses with blinders. It makes us believe the light at the end of the tunnel is the only truth out there, instead of realizing there are more tunnels to be explored."

She nodded and laughed a bit, "Mr. Worship, was it? How profound of you to say. Are you American, too?"

"Naturalized, yes," he answered upon returning the pistol to her, "But does it matter? This wager. This weapon. This vehicle. You and I. Him and them. We're all data in the eyes of science. We're all equal values in information and in truth. It has nothing to do with affiliation or background."

With renewed peace in her heart, she approached Ruiz, "This isn't the way the game should be played. My deepest apologies for resorting to such tactics. Please, I'll do what I can to help."

"We'll talk," the valet responded without looking at her, "when the most excellent captain heals. I have no gratitude to convey, Ms. Plain."

As soon as the doctor permitted Azuchi to be moved, he asked Worship and his assistants to accompany her, signifying his desire to remain in Hyde Park.

"Airi, please be safe. I know for certain, you'll live a fruitful life," he whispered before she was taken away, "There's no need to wait. My debts to society I shall repay in due time."

"Wait! Chotto matte!" she bawled upon seeing Ruiz stay, "You can't do this to me! Shicha dame!"

Nonetheless, there was nothing much she could do. When the carriage had left, the former soldier carefully slipped into the motivated crowds to proceed to the stage, in case his master needed his services for one last time. There was Haze, receiving the plaudits of all, while he invited Minerva Rausch to share the spotlight with him. Apparently, the Austrian singer was among the crowds who helped carry the British gentleman to complete his journey. Holding her hand again for the first time since leaving Panama gave a nostalgic feel. It was as if they were apart years ago.

They were on top of the world. A dream of dreams. Haze, for making good on his pledge to demonstrate that the state of global progress could make it possible to tour the world in less than 80 days. Rausch, for being a good sportswoman. The fact that she accommodated the gentleman did not fall into deaf ears. Indeed, the news of the collaboration spread like wildfire. What many did not know was Haze's conviction not to cross any British nor American territory. If observers would be able to sort that out, what else could they do? When all was said and done, the magnanimous Haze also called for the third competitor, Jane Plain, to join them. The people were initially uncertain on how to treat the person who almost killed their champion, but when Haze decided to vouch for her as a worthy opponent, the audiences began to accept her as well.

Besides the 60,000 pounds originally set aside as the jackpot, the representative with them verified that winnings would further be compounded by commissions from promoting the competition and by the wagers made by those who attempted to predict the return date. Of the millions of tickets sold around the world, there were only two who correctly predicted the homecoming on Day 72. This was because the betting outlets, out of insistent demand, also allowed calling the right hour and minute of return. Theoretically speaking, the challenge meant guessing from more than 100,000 possible answers. All accounted for, the winner would receive at least 120,000 pounds. During his circumnavigation, Haze also managed to broker deals that helped ease his expenses. Despite his immense spending, he still had a net gain of 4,000 pounds without any bank withdrawals.

As the representative was about to hand over two bagful of prize money, a uniformed officer fired a warning shot in the air, "Let not the exchange continue! Chief Inspector I. M. Portrade, Scotland Yard! Here to apprehend Mr. Richard Haze in the name of Her Majesty!"

Taking his precipitous declaration as their clear and definite signal to act, the constables swiftly broke through the bewildered crowds to take away the accused gentleman. Their organization demolished the earlier resistance which Haze's supporters audaciously built.

"He's the man who robbed the Bank of England!" Portrade continued, "Mr. Haze has done a great disservice to the empire! We shall work on revoking his entire—"

"This is wrong! Sir Haze is beyond reproach!" Ruiz stretched his arms to hinder the constables from arresting his master, "He's not the one who stole the money!"

"Oh, are you not Haze's valet?" the chief inspector remarked while rubbing his moustache, "If not your gentleman, then who did the deed?"

The former soldier looked at Haze, who slightly shook his head, before turning back to Portrade and to the people, "It is I, Corporal Juan Ruiz! I thieved the Bank of England of 110,000 pounds to finance the revolution in

Filipinas! Yes, I robbed a colonial power to topple another colonizer! Know this, people of Great Britain! Freedom is not free! It comes with a price we Filipinos are more than ready to render! Blood! Toil! Sweat! Tears!"

"Oh, alright. Shut up. If it's truly an alien like you who robbed the bank, then it'd make my task easier," the chief inspector waved his hand, "Enough chat and come with us peacefully."

"If you'll excuse us, Mr. Haze!" Portrade yelled at the competitors on stage, "With the real thief surfacing, I'll ensure all charges against you are dropped! Are we good? Congratulations!"

While Ruiz gave back the travel bags of his master, dropped his weapons, and offered his empty hands to the authorities, the constables nevertheless did not take any chances, especially those who saw him in combat against Plain and Azuchi. No less than 20 of them accompanied the handcuffed penitent to incarcerate him. Haze was placed in a quandary. His valet had cleared him of all suspicions, firm on the resolve that he would take the fall for all his sins. As much as he wanted to rescue his friend right there and then, he was soon drowned by continuous applause from the audience, and flooded by media personnel who sought his answers on a myriad of issues, including the latest developments on the bank robbery.

"Richard, what's happening?" Rausch went close to the gentleman for him to hear, "Why did they arrest him instead?"

"I can't explain this now, Minerva," Haze motioned for her to act ignorant, "Ich habe volles Vertrauen zu ihm."

For the rest of the day, Ruiz was not interrogated in prison. He was given no attention at all, depriving him of the most basic food and water requirements. He languished in his cell, which despite being upgraded to "humane standards", was still less cozy than a cramped apartment block in the industrial zones. It would only be the following day when the interrogation began, and the former soldier was only too happy to tell them everything, from the lapse in bank security to his operations outside Britain. He was committed to let all he carried to this stage go.

Beyond his knowledge, Her Majesty's Government began to communicate the latest revelation to Spain. Since they had no way to restore the funds stolen by Ruiz, no matter how much they pressured him to churn out the amount, the British leaders thought they could try recovering at least part of it by extraditing the accused to Spain, since it was customary for the demanding authority to shoulder the costs of extradition. The British would be cleared of any responsibility in dealing with his case, and they gained favor with Spain.

The victor of the wager, meanwhile, did not rest after his phenomenal win. He did not take time to enjoy his stupendous triumph. He went to all people in high places he could discuss with concerning Ruiz's situation, including the Governor of the Bank of England and the Prime Minister. However, not even his pledge of investing 110,000 pounds to replenish what the Filipino revolutionary robbed did not persuade his peers in the Reform Club. Haze may be the darling of the public now, but none in Her Majesty's Government would like to decide quite immediately. After all, Ruiz admitted to have rebelled against his nation's colonial masters. If Britain would allow such a dangerous person to be freed, would not that be a subtle endorsement for their own colonies to overthrow the foreigner's yoke as well? In addition, Haze had already been absolved of harboring a revolutionary after Scotland Yard shifted the blame on the valet services for failing to do proper background checks. If the gentleman would insist on interfering into the case further, he was warned about potential repercussions that might sully his globally-acclaimed victory.

It took an entire week before the Spanish government officially responded, on March 21. Apparently, there was another change of government in the Peninsula. King Amadeo abdicated the throne on February 11, three weeks after the foiled revolution in Manila. Replacing him was President Estanislao Figueras, a lawyer turned politician, and a staunch advocate of republicanism. Faced with economic recession, political fragmentation, riots in Madrid, federalists in Catalan, and rebels in Cuba, among others, the new head of state did not seek to add the extradition of a troublesome Filipino revolutionary to his daily problems. Alaminos's exaggerated reports on the short-lived uprising already alarmed the Spanish government of the impeccable timing of Filipino nationalists. If he were allowed to set foot on Spain, Ruiz might be transformed into an additional rallying point of discontented elements in the Peninsula, considering how he also espoused republican and democratic ideals, at least publicly speaking. Not even his execution would be sufficient to silence his cause.

In sum, the Spanish concluded to keep a hands-off policy on Ruiz, presenting reports from the Philippines that the revolutionary leader was presumed dead. Allegedly credible testimonies were conveniently gathered to support this belief. Owing to scant information available, there was no feasible method to verify if their current prisoner was a faker or the real deal. They also downplayed his role as merely one of the sub-leaders, rather than the mastermind, just as they also minimized the extent of the revolution closest to overthrowing their longstanding rule at the very heart of the Philippines. Besides, the name Juan Ruiz was common in the Spanish dominions. One could probably find a person named Ruiz for every 100 Spaniards or so. It was probably as common as the surname Smith in England. This infuriated British officials. They realized their schemes backfired against them. Figueras intelligently toyed with the legal details to shame Her Majesty's Government. Perhaps the only saving grace was how the said communications were kept only between them.

The following day, Haze was startled to receive in his home a visit from the Prime Minister himself, who was modestly dressed to avoid attention. With him was the commissioner of Scotland Yard, still embarrassed at his initial accusations against the gentleman. Upon welcoming them in and quickly serving them, a routine he had been quite accustomed to since winning the wager, both officials marveled at the scientific innovations around. They also hinted a possible knighthood from the Queen, before proceeding to the reason for the meet.

"Let's get to brass tacks, shall we?" the seated Prime Minister massaged his temple, "I believe prudence, not fear, ought to precede any decision. Our commissioner here can attest how I judged you not when it came to the bank robbery question."

As Scotland Yard's head nodded quite energetically, the Prime Minister continued, "Since your valet, if he was truly one in the first place, admitted to the crime, we're at a loss on how to deal with his case. The Spanish government refused extradition, and we can't hold him on trial either."

"Right Honorable," Haze sarcastically remarked, "If you were not as abrupt in arresting the culprit, you won't have to face this dilemma, correct?"

Britain's head of government sighed, "Please allow us to accept your offer to deposit in the Bank of England. We have seen the wisdom on the proposal we earlier rejected."

"What's in it for me?" the gentleman cleaned his glasses, "Wouldn't the banks in France, Switzerland, or the United States even, be better options to invest my hard-earned money?"

The commissioner scoffed, pointing a finger at Haze, "Hard-earned? That's bull! Where is your heart of nationalism? Be grateful and give back to the people the money you gained from them!"

"You're the fraudsters!" the wager's victor blurted out, "You say some reformers were too radical? Alright! You say other reformers dream too much? Touche! But how have your own reforms benefited the people? At this point, Germany and the United States are about to overtake our industrial production! Russia, China, and Japan are not far behind as you'd want to believe! Why should I refrain from being generous to those who seek progress? If Britain shall embark on such a path, I'll gladly contribute without coercion!"

"Richard, let's calm our nerves," the Prime Minister slightly raised his hands, "Commissioner, you understand we're here to enlist Mr. Haze's assistance. Restrain your sharp tongue, if you may."

"You still haven't answered my query," Haze stood up and reached for his cane.

"We'll arrange," the Prime Minister cleared his throat as he carefully chose his words, "for the release and the citizenship of Juan Ruiz on two conditions. First is your deposit with the Bank of England. Second is your mutual agreement to recognize the cessation of his existence. This exchange never happened as far as everyone is concerned."

"He's already dead. What else would you seek? Against whom will you blame the robbery?"

"We have weighed the situation. A patsy is ready. What we seek is your agreement. We can have you escorted in the event you decide invest the money today."

A few taps of the cane closed the deal. It was the minimum outcome Haze intended to achieve in the first place, and he was internally happy that his better judgment got into them. Besides the escort sent by Scotland Yard, the British gentleman was also chaperoned by Rausch. While she was quite jealous that

Haze decided not to invest much of the winnings on her own chain of banks, the Austrian singer was overjoyed to hear what he said in the presence of the media covering his trip to the Bank of England.

"You might think I gave up my treasure to what was recently proven as one of the less secure banks in the world," he snickered, "But fear not! I discovered that true treasure lies where my heart is, and none could hope to replace it. Therefore, I announce my intention to formally pursue the hand of the dearest Freiin to be my lifetime security. Ich liebe dich, Minerva Rausch."

"Sir Richard Haze! I thought you'd never!" the baroness excitedly held the gentleman by the arm, "Ich liebe dich auch."

A baroness and a soon-to-be knight! The Bank of England witnessed thereafter an impromptu live performance from the overjoyed Rausch, expressing her happiness through song. Haze, while eager to sing with her back in Panama, was embarrassed to do so in Britain. The best he could muster was to gallantly hold her as she performed. Whether it was a genuine whirlwind romance or a union of sociopolitical convenience, an Austrian lady and a British gentleman being together would be a foreign policy gift to Her Majesty's Government, yet as much as he had already benefited the nation, Britain had yet to fulfill their part of the deal. On the same day, two hours before midnight, Haze, his good friend Fogg, and Captain Azuchi visited the jail where Ruiz was supposedly incarcerated. It took some time before the warden himself attended to them.

"Gentlemen and lady, my dear guests!" he nervously opened as he brought out Ruiz's sabre and pistol, "I can't fathom how it happened, but the prisoner is gone!"

"Your man of confidence is quite a puzzle, is he not?" the now healthy Fogg calmly remarked, "If he were in the service of Scotland Yard—"

Azuchi, however, was not convinced of the revelation, "Gone?! Don't tell me you killed him!"

A prison guard brought out a white shirt with words written in red, presumably blood, "We found this in his cell, but not even his shadow remained. He disappeared without a trace."

They examined the shirt, which bore a Latin phrase. *Illum oportet crescere me autem minui*. That is, he must become greater, I must become less. It was an allusion to the Bible, but none of them understood the message in their present context. Following it was a Filipino phrase. *Hiraya manawari*. What the Japanese captain could confirm was that it was indeed Ruiz's writing. The warden, meanwhile, gave assurances that no execution was done. In fact, they were appreciative of him. The former soldier turned out to be one of the most cooperative prisoners they had in quite some time. He spilled everything without hesitation, and the conviction in his statements persuaded that he had no reason to lie. He even gave subtle recommendations on improving security.

"If he's dead," Fogg quipped, "you won't be too rattled on finding excuses, yes?"

"Yet, he broke out of *your* prison, is that what you're getting at?" Haze finally spoke, "If a solitary… Filipino, was it? If he could break into the Bank of England and escape from prison–"

"I'll surely find him!" Azuchi clenched her fists, her wound seemingly unable to bother her at this point, "And when I do, he'll get the beating of a lifetime!"

"Can you refresh my memory?" Ruiz's erstwhile master turned to her, "How did you meet him?"

"Haze-san," she closed her eyes as she pacified her spirit, "there is much to say about Risu Tsuringu. My admiration for him was sparked only a year ago, but how can I hope to begin?"

Thus, the person who vowed to continue the revolution, and left his opportunity to lead a simple and peaceful life, had officially ceased to exist in this world. With his whereabouts unknown, and his motivations enigmatic, one could only speculate what could have occurred after this. He was known by many names. He entered many occupations. Juan Ruiz. John Ruy. Juan Pasaporte. Fuan Xiansheng. Joseph Smith. Risu Tsuringu. Who knew what other identity had the Filipino assumed in the eternal search for his life's purpose? On the other hand, who could say they had not attempted to wear different masks depending on the situation? Who had been consistent enough in every aspect?

Was it their own choice, or was it the system which compelled them to develop various personalities? What could have justified living such double lives, if it was truly justifiable to begin with? If we learn to trust and communicate with each other better, would such barriers and misunderstandings dissolve? Or would we be able to find more ways to enter conflict, as if humanity was cursed to viciously fight and thanklessly strive forever? When would it end? Perhaps, it was truly love and war of all against all.

Epilogue: Cruel Angel's Thesis

"Arriving at J. Ruiz Station! Paparating na sa J. Ruiz Station!"

A Filipino student emerged on the platform of the Light Rail Transit (LRT) with phone in hand, recording herself as she delivered a part of her thesis presentation in class the following day. What had she written about? It turned out to be the story of Juan Ruiz, the gentleman thief of the Bank of England who led a revolution in Manila, and circumnavigated the world in 72 days. Her study was so extensive, she managed to find Samuel's grave in the Chinese cemetery as well.

"Contrary to popular belief," she enthusiastically said in front of her professor and her classmates, "The street J. Ruiz was actually named after this man. He's Rizal true inspiration. Not even Bonifacio nor Aguinaldo managed to get so close in taking over Manila, but he did. Almost. 150 years ago."

"Miss, where'd you get this? Social media? This is a research class. I know Burgos. I know the Cavite Mutiny. I even know Wakanda," her professor leaned, his hand supporting his head, "But if you're so intent on spouting all these fantastically weaved stories, better take fiction writing."

"Sir, this isn't fake news!" she shook her hands, "It's a family tradition passed on to generations! Our clan supported efforts to rename the street. My grandfather's grandfather was an eyewitness account. He's a primary source."

"Ito naman ang sabi ng lolo ng lolo ko," the professor stood up, "Preposterous! We know Juan Ruiz was one of the first casualties of the 1896 Philippine Revolution. There's no record of your 1873. It doesn't mean that if it runs in the family, it's true. Get your facts straight, please. We don't need a Majoha moment here, miss. What's the name of your ancestor anyway?"

"I know it's Gomburza. But okay, I understand, sir," she closed her presentation and bowed, quite convinced that there was no way for her to change minds regardless of what evidence she had, "I'm sorry for taking your time. I'll make a new thesis right away."

"No, no. We're already there," he laughed, "Just humor me. Who's that primary source?"

The student sighed, thinking he would insult her more, "One of Ruiz's allies, Raul Gonzalez."

The professor burst out laughing, louder than he had previously done, and the class followed, although some of them were oblivious to the reason behind the seemingly uncalled for reaction. Apparently, his mind immediately connected Ruiz and Gonzalez as members of the football team Real Madrid. She was, however, not making any sports references.

The student learned from family stories and local tradition of Raul Gonzalez being the mercenary leader from San Juan who fought with *El Tulisan* Casimiro Camerino and *El Presidente* Juan Ruiz. The narrow street today was formerly the site of his demolished home. Conventional knowledge, meanwhile, failed to uphold her cause. At the end of the day, the student was forced to write on a new thesis topic, but with considerably less time. She could only hope to pass.

So much about a revolution in 80 days.

About the Author

Arius Lauren Raposas

With a heart to honor God and the people, Arius Lauren Raposas has faithfully served in the executive and the legislative branches of government in the Philippines. He finished a bachelor's degree in history (magna cum laude) and a master's degree in public administration (thesis track) at the University of the Philippines Diliman. Besides his academic and research work, he has authored a number of literary works through the years, a roster that includes Code Antony (2010), Run to the Sky (2017), Countdown to Inferno (2020), Kotabahara: The City of God (2020), Muni: Dream Princess (2020), and this book you now possess. He has shared knowledge related to his expertise through national and international media appearances. In addition, he has established presence in social media, where his history website called Filipino Historian (2012) reaches an average of around a million people each day.

www.ingramcontent.com/pod-product-compliance
Lightning Source LLC
LaVergne TN
LVHW041914070526
838199LV00051BA/2608